THE Wanton Widow

The Scandalous Sisters

HELENE MATHESON

OLIVERHEBERBOOKS

For all the women who agree with Reese Witherspoon,
The Scandalous Sisters will never ask a man,
"What should we do now?"

Prologue

Lady Phoebe,

I am ~~aroused beyond measure~~ honoured by your faith in me. Please trust in my conviction to serve you ~~well with my cock~~ and know that I would never cause any damage upon your reputation, nor would I allow another to impugn your character.

I have obtained the literature you requested ~~and memorized every single page~~ without incident. Lord Astley was extremely curious, ~~however, not as much as I~~ as to which one of my clients requested it. Fortunately, I was able to assure him he was not familiar with the young ~~delectable widow~~ married nobleman I represented, ~~if he was, I would plant a facer on his lordship~~. My response seemed to satisfy him and he was more than happy to assist another gentleman to obtain, as he stated, "Unparalleled bliss." ~~In my case, abject torture.~~ He would, *however, like the book returned to him once the ~~lady of my every desire~~ gentleman has achieved his goals.*

Since receiving your letter, I have found myself ~~harder than the nude marble statue in the great hall of Caerlaverock Castle~~ in a most uncomfortable state on a nightly basis. I hope that you can forgive my ~~debauchery~~ forwardness, but I feel we have come to a place in our relationship that my question must finally be asked, if not in person, ~~because I do not trust myself not to bury my face under your skirts the moment you whisper, "Yes,"~~ then in written correspondence: Why have you not asked for my guidance? I would gladly introduce you to "unparalleled bliss."

~~I beg of you to end this misery~~ Your servant in every request,

Joshua Forrester, Esquire

—A very inappropriate letter drafted by Joshua Forrester, Esquire to his employer Lady Phoebe Drake. He rewrote the letter before sending the entirely scandalous final version. February 1811

Lady Phoebe Drake had teased him in his dreams for as long as he could remember. And as she stood across the ballroom of Drake Manor staring in his direction with those gorgeous eyes, her tongue swiped her lower lip. To every other man in the room, it was the act of a practiced coquette. Her man of affairs, Joshua Forrester, however, knew the opposite to be true.

She was nervous beyond compare. A barely-there-tic in her right cheek displayed how much her act of seduction was costing her. Phoebe's gaze suddenly went beyond her target and fell upon him, and for a moment she froze, despite still moving in his direction.

Then her luminescent green eyes refocused on the other man. The man whom she planned to seduce. Taller and broader than himself, the Duke of Ross was her mark for this evening and Joshua couldn't stop the growl from rising in his throat as he watched Phoebe's demeanor soften. Yet despite the flirtation in her eyes, he recognized the manner in which she bolstered her armor. She'd been putting on this show for years. She was genuinely nervous. This game they played involved high stakes, which seemed to heighten the sense of adventure in her eyes. She had a purpose she was determined to see through to the end, despite the danger.

Joshua watched from outside the ballroom doors as the sway of her hips mesmerized every man who laid eyes upon her. The way her gown hugged her luscious curves was like an invitation he wanted to answer "God, yes, please and thank you." Instead, he kept to the shadows and watched as she lured the Duke of Ross to his downfall.

When she arrived at the duke's side, Phoebe held herself with the decorum of a queen as Ross bowed, reached for her gloved hand and brushed his lips across her knuckles. Ross's gaze traveled up her body and held on her breasts longer than acceptable. It made Joshua want to blacken his eyes, make them to swell closed and temporarily blind the man. He pushed open the doors to the ballroom just a crack in order to hear their conversation.

"Lady Drake, you look absolutely delectable in that gown," Ross said.

Phoebe blushed, genuine embarrassment filling her cheeks as color traveled down her neck and to her breasts, which Ross continued to openly admire. Yet despite her embarrassment, Phoebe pushed through her nervous state and leaned in closer, requiring Ross to bend over for her to whisper into his ear. "I have found that I very much like to be a man's dessert."

Bloody hell. He wanted dessert. Whose blasted idea was this?

Her gaze flickered in his direction, as if guilt lay behind the flirtatious smile she delivered to the duke, and Joshua had to remind himself that it was just a ruse. The duke would not be bedding Phoebe. Ross just needed to *believe* it would be Phoebe in his bed, instead of her cousin.

He had no idea why Phoebe thought this would work. Beyond sharing the same hair and eye color, her cousin looked nothing like her. Phoebe was all dips and curves, and more curves he wanted to run his tongue over. His cock twitched at the thought of taking the soft round globes of her arse in his hands. He wanted her legs wrapped around his waist when he lifted her and drove his cock into her sweet cunny.

Her cousin brought none of that to mind.

Phoebe had a passionate nature she held in check. She knew how to flirt, of that there was no doubt, but none of these men had unleashed the hellcat within. They witnessed the image she portrayed to the *ton*. Her wanton way was in her walk, and in the manner in which she carried herself with a born assurance of her allure, something her cousin lacked. Maturity gave Phoebe the ability to command any room as if she were the lady of the castle. Her home was luxurious, but it did not come close to the opulence of her cousin's estate, yet anyone who saw the two women together would believe Phoebe held the higher station in the ton, not the other way around.

Dressed in an elegant navy blue silk confection that hugged her in all the right places, she was the perfect image of femininity. As her skirts swished, every man in the room stared at her arse as if they too wanted to run their tongue over her perfect lily-white bottom. And if her arse didn't grab their attention, her cleavage made other fantasies come to mind. Like the dream he'd suffered through the previous night as he'd pushed the length of his cock in between her ample breasts to her lips.

Blast. He needed to stop thinking of every position he wanted to take her. Even the cold February night did nothing to stop his arousal from straining the front of his trousers. He pushed his erection down and concentrated on what was occurring inside the ballroom.

The back of the duke's hand grazed down Phoebe's arm, his shameless display causing her to flinch and a couple of the ladies to gasp. He may as well have branded her a whore.

Joshua's lip curled into a sneer. He'd kill the man, duke or no duke. No one had the right to openly brand a woman in such a manner. He reached for the door just as Phoebe stepped back and pushed it closed as she smacked the duke's hand with her fan. "You grow too bold, Your Grace," she stated with a resounding finality that carried through the door, and he knew her warning also applied him.

She winked at the duke and licked her lips in a practice as old as time before she whispered the message she was meant to deliver. Joshua knew she would invite Ross to meet her in the garden in thirty minutes. That was the plan, and it was up to Phoebe to deliver the invitation and then extract herself from the duke before he could change the location. The temperatures didn't make it an ideal location for a seduction, but it was the only place guaranteed not to have light. It was imperative the duke believe he was making love to Phoebe, and not another woman altogether.

With her invitation delivered, Phoebe glided across the room to a group of ladies standing by the fire. The ladies turned in unison to gaze in the duke's direction. Their expressions an array of scorn, disdain, ridicule...and interest. He would never understand the ladies of the ton who regarded women with censure while being thoroughly engrossed in the scandal of it all. Ross raised his glass to toast the ladies before downing his brandy, and Joshua knew that was his signal to leave.

He made his way across the balcony and into the library, each step bringing him closer to the woman he wanted more than any other. Phoebe would not be the duke's partner tonight. She would be his once and for all. He was done playing the cordial man of affairs she could keep at arm's length. They were meant to be together. He was too old to play these games of cat and mouse. She needed to let go of her fears, and he planned to help her choose him over anyone else.

It was time for *unparalleled bliss*.

Lady Phoebe Drake was going to be sick. She hurried down the hallway, the plush carpet masking her quick retreat as she pushed open the library door and slipped inside, quietly shutting the door behind her. She leaned back against the door as she inhaled through her nose and exhaled through her lips. "Just breathe, Phoebe. Breathe," she whispered.

Every house party she'd ever thrown had ended with her casting up her accounts. Acting like a whore was not in her nature, yet she had no one else to blame but herself. She had started this masquerade to get back at a man, believing it would get easier with each passing year. Clearly, she'd been wrong.

This time, however, she'd done it for a good cause. Her cousin needed to seduce the Duke of Ross. Her reasoning was complicated, but understandable. Besides, wasn't there a heavy price for every worthwhile act? She hoped she'd just paid the heavy price, and from here, the task would get easier. Once the deed was done, she could disappear from society and focus on her millinery business. She didn't want this scandalous life any longer. It was time to return to her roots. It was the only true answer to where she belonged.

"You did wonderfully," a deep voice rumbled from across the room, interrupting her reverie.

Phoebe jumped and put her hand to her chest as she stared at the one man who invoked the type of passion she'd just pretended to feel. His tall, lean frame lounged against her desk with his arms and ankles crossed in a casual display of power. His attire wasn't as expensive as Ross's, but his buff breaches, and waist coat with his navy jacket fit him just as well, perhaps better. His dark eyes drew her in, but it was his mouth that always seemed to capture her imagination. She'd dreamed of what he could do with those lips, but ever since she'd read the books he'd acquired for her, his tongue had played a larger role.

Lord, forgive her, but this man made her thoughts turn utterly lustful.

He held a glass of brandy in one hand that was half full. He turned and picked up a second glass from her desk, and held it out to her. She smiled and walked towards him, conscious of the sway of her hips and the way he devoured her progress with one chestnut lock falling across his forehead. His gaze slowly traveled down the length of her as if he were savoring every step she took, and her body instantly heated.

"I thought I was going to be sick all over the ballroom floor," she confessed.

"Has that happened before?"

"Not in front of anyone, but when the night winds down and I'm able to escape..." She shrugged. "It seems I was not born for the stage."

"And yet you've put on that show countless times. I'd wager tonight, however, was your best performance. Are you going to be sick now?"

She cocked her head and realized the urge to cast up her accounts was gone. It had been replaced with a much more enticing nervous energy. "No. Surprisingly, I'm not." She accepted the glass he proffered and took a sip of the amber liquid, savoring the taste before swallowing. "I think he fell for it."

"He did. I watched him head towards the garden before I came here." Forrester emptied his glass in one gulp and set it down behind him on the desk before taking her glass and placing it next to his. Then he took her hand and held it in his own as he turned it over, leisurely studying it as if it were a museum piece at which to marvel. Slowly, he undid the buttons at her elbow one by one, the movement casual, yet tantalizing with every delicate touch.

Who knew such strong and powerful hands could be so gentle. He proceeded to push the glove down and her breath hitched as his bare hand ran a path down her forearm. Never before had the act of removing her gloves been erotic, yet with Joshua's touch it was so much more.

He looked up into her eyes, trapping her in a web of seduction she didn't want to escape as he pulled her glove off one finger at a time. His gaze never leaving hers as he dropped the ivory satin glove on the desktop and brought her hand to his lips. She became fascinated by the tantalizing caress of his warm breath on each of her fingers, a precursor to the true temptation of desire that assaulted her as he bestowed each with a reverent kiss.

"What are you doing?" she finally asked as he reached for her other hand and removed her second glove in the same seductive manner.

"I made you a promise I plan to keep." He brought her second hand up to his lips and repeated the intimate caresses once more.

Phoebe found it difficult to breathe. Her chest rose and fell in a pace that was unseemly. She was losing her composure rather quickly. "I don't remember you making any promises."

It was a lie. She knew exactly what promise he had made to her.

How did this man wield such power over her restraint? He exposed a part of her she wasn't certain she wanted to acknowledge. Admitting to the thrill his dominance elicited went against everything she had become in the last decade. It was like succumbing to a husband, something she swore she would never do. This side of Joshua inflamed and scared her just the same. It was humbling to realize she wanted to take a leap of faith and give in to his allure.

"You know exactly what promise I made," he said, and he began kissing along her hand to her wrist where he focused on the erratic thump of her pulse. Then he gently sucked on her flesh as he looked up into her eyes. "Unparalleled bliss."

"I believe that was the Earl of Astley's promise," she whispered.

"He said the book would give a gentleman unparalleled bliss. I promised to give it to *you*."

Oh, how she wanted the bliss he promised. Her nipples hardened and she felt warm heat between her legs as her body prepared for him to make good on his vow. Yet something inside her wanted to flee. She forced the next statement from her lips. "I'm not certain that's a good idea."

Even as she said it, she found herself stepping into his arms and putting her bare hands to the front of his cold coat. Despite the layers of clothing that separated their flesh, strong, hard muscle met her touch.

"You're freezing. We should move closer to the fire." She began to pull away, but his hands immediately locked on her lower back and held her in place.

"I'm burning up for you."

He pulled her against his strong masculine form, and suddenly she felt the heat he was talking about pushing into her stomach, long and hard. She nearly moaned at the idea of him being so aroused.

She'd always found his scent intoxicating. A mixture of something fresh and earthy, sandalwood and the essence of Joshua. Spicy and male, this evening it fused with the aroma of the best brandy she owned, adding up to something irresistible that was reserved just for him. Her breath caught, and her gaze slipped to the mouth she'd admired for too many years.

It was all the invitation Joshua needed as he slowly bent down and pressed his lips to hers for the first time. It was like nothing she had ever experienced.

She forgot about the party that was going on in her ballroom, even the plight of her cousin was lost to his kiss. The heat between them was instant. Combustible. It was the promise she'd whispered in the ears of so many men without ever delivering. Not once had she ever experienced a kiss like Joshua's.

Suddenly he was spinning her around as graceful as a waltz on the dance floor and her backside was against her desk as she got lost in their all-consuming passion. He tasted of brandy and something so erotic she couldn't put a name to it, but it was all man, all Joshua.

When his tongue brushed her lips in a silent plea to let him in, she opened to him and allowed the kiss to deepen. She'd heard women discuss kisses that had made them senseless, yet she had never understood the meaning...until Joshua. He aroused something in her that no other man had come close to touching.

Desire stormed through her body as his hands traced her hips before traveling down to her buttocks to knead her flesh. He groaned into their kiss as something unleashed within him. Phoebe found herself on top of her desk with her skirts pulled up to her thighs and Joshua spreading her legs wide for him to step between. Then his hands were in her hair, pulling pins and disheveling her coiffure as her untamed curls dropped to her shoulders.

The hard ridge of his cock strained against his falls as it met the soft folds of her undergarments where she pulsed with need. His delicious kiss was consuming her. She tore at his jacket, desperate to feel more of him as his manhood grew harder, longer. She could feel the alluring length of his sex demanding satisfaction, and the wetness at the juncture of her thighs prepared her for the experience he'd promised as his mouth ravaged hers.

Until the clock struck the hour and reality came crashing in. She pulled back from his kiss and he stopped. Their chests rising and falling as if they'd run all the way from the estate gates.

"We must stop."

"No," he breathed and dipped his head to kiss her once more.

She leaned back, pulling away from the kiss she wanted with all of her being. "I have to go get her; Ross will be waiting."

"Let him wait." His hands gripped her buttocks and he started to pull her closer, but she pushed against his chest and kept him at arm's length despite her desire to feed the craving he'd awakened within her.

She peered into his intense, hooded gaze. "You don't understand. He is a duke. Ross will not wait. She must get there now. If she is late, he will leave."

Joshua closed his eyes and sighed before he released her and stepped out from between her thighs, his gaze lost to the place where his body had abandoned her own.

Phoebe quickly pulled her skirts down over her knees, her cheeks reddening as he helped her down from the desk. How had this happened? How had she forgotten the reason they were here? This wasn't about the passion between them. This was about a woman's future. Her cousin's livelihood depended on her meeting the Duke of Ross in the garden.

"Don't," he said.

"Don't what?" She brushed the front of her gown, attempting, and failing to remove the wrinkles their passion created.

"Don't sully what just happened between us in your mind. We are consenting adults."

"You don't understand," she said as she picked up several pins from the desktop and began arranging her hair the best she could.

Joshua picked up her drink and downed it before saying, "Then help me to understand."

"I cannot let her down. I know what it's like to have a man control one's future. To depend on him to make plans for one's financial stability. I trusted my father to do what was best for me, and he left the business to my husband. I trusted Richard to do what was best for me, and he drove Lady Atwood's Millinery into the ground with his mismanagement. I knew how to run the business but he refused to ask me for help. Then he died leaving me with nothing. You of all people know the financial straits I was in at the time of his death.

"No woman should have to live with the threat of debtor's prison, working on her back, or living on the streets because her husband refused to acknowledge she knew more about business than he did."

Joshua ran a hand through his hair. "You're right. I know how hard you worked to restore your family business. No one should be kept in the dark about something as important as their safety and security."

She smiled at him ruefully. "Of course you do. I'm sorry. I just can't let the same thing happen to my cousin that happened to me."

"There is no need to apologize. The three of us planned for this night, and we will see it through. Together. As a team."

She couldn't believe her ears. He truly was the best of men. "We will meet you at the servant's entrance. Then you can escort her through the back gate of the garden."

"And once she is with him? Can I come to your room?"

The idea was so very tempting...but if he had taught her anything, it was that she couldn't trust herself with him. Because when his lips met hers, she had relinquished every bit of her control over to him, and that was a mistake she would never make again. "Let us ensure that she secures her future and then we will talk."

Phoebe rushed out the library door without looking back. She didn't want to fall prey to his charms and the promise of what being with Joshua could be like. She had no doubt the experience would be life altering, and she didn't think she was ready to relinquish control of her future to any man.

One

Lady Phoebe,

I ~~would be most pleased~~ apologize if my behavior ~~aroused you beyond measure~~ offended you in any way. I believed my actions to not only be what you needed, but what you desired. ~~I certainly did.~~ I was driven by my ~~cock~~ commitment to please you in all that I do, not what I failed to do. ~~Because I apparently failed to do it rather miserably.~~

If I had not served as your ~~sounding board, confidant, partner in crime~~ solicitor for so many years, I might be prone to believe your ~~escape~~ departure from ~~the house party~~ in London was ~~out of fear of me and what I planned for that evening~~ due to a desire to retire to the country for a few months ~~in hiding~~ respite.

I was pleased to hear your cousin had come to terms with the duke. It is the appropriate, and best outcome for

*all involved. Our results, however...damnation woman,
you left me with an unending cockstand I cannot satisfy
and I strongly suspect your sweet cunny is dripping as you
read this. I have been everything that is proper, but we are
not proper. We are debauched, depraved, and downright
dirty. Our minds have been in the gutters for months. I
know I am not alone in this wickedness. You were
grinding your delightful quim against my cock and you
nearly unmanned me in your library.*

*Ross is coming for the duchess, and my dear Lady, I
am coming for you. I have spent years waiting for you,
and I will not give up on us now when we are so close to the
unparalleled bliss I promised.*

*Your servant in every request,
Joshua*

*—A very inappropriate letter from Joshua Forrester,
Esquire to Lady Phoebe Drake. He began to correct his
unseemly desires with a more discrete correspondence, but
then decided to hell with it, he was done pretending. He
sent the correspondence as drafted April 1811*

Lady Phoebe Drake sat at the dressing table in the guest room of Caerlaverock Castle staring at the letter in her hand. This room had been her sanctuary in the family wing when she visited Caerlaverock since before the Duchess of Nithesdale was a duchess. Before she and Iseabail were scandalous beyond redemption thanks to Iseabail's late husband, the Duke of Nithesdale.

"What does it say?" Iseabail asked.

"Pardon?" Phoebe's voice sounded strangled to her own ears.

"The letter. It must be bad news, your face has lost all its color."

The attention to the letter in her lap made her coloring return ten-fold, as if she'd stoked the flames in the hearth into a blazing bonfire.

"Ohh." Iseabail grinned. "It's that kind of letter."

"No, really it's nothing of import." She lied.

"How can you say that when your blush says the exact opposite?"

Phoebe folded the letter and shoved it up her sleeve. "Given the situation we currently face, I hardly find this missive a topic for us to concern ourselves with."

"Yet I find it exactly what I need to distract me from my *current* circumstances." She unconsciously rubbed her rounded baby bump as if the child in her womb needed to know it was loved—the child was Iseabail's world, it was loved beyond measure.

The circling of Iseabail's hand caused another pang of longing for a child Phoebe would never have. She sighed and rubbed her temple above her right eye as she confessed, "It's from Forrester."

"I knew it!" Iseabail exclaimed.

"You knew nothing of the sort. He wrote it months ago."

Iseabail's hand paused. "Months? When?"

Phoebe found herself confessing to only one of Joshua's secret letters that she'd received, and it wasn't this one.

"When I asked him to assist with the acquirement of *The Memoirs of a Wanton Woman.*"

Iseabail's breath caught. "I still can't believe you did that, yet I have to admit, I had assumed you obtained them from your husband's library."

She shook her head and attempted to smile but failed. "Richard was not that interested in marital relations."

"Oh, I'm sorry."

"The last thing I want is your pity. Our marriage was very pleasant."

Iseabail coughed as if *pleasant* was unimaginable. She supposed it would be to someone who'd only experienced the type of riveting passion Iseabail had experienced with the father of her child, but for most marriages of the ton, pleasant was as good as it got. Phoebe had never had any complaints about any of the aspects of her marriage, until after Richard's death. The financial state he had left her in, however, had painted their relationship in an altogether different light.

Yet her viewpoint towards marital relations had never changed—until she read Joshua's letter that accompanied the bawdy books she'd requested he obtain. His letter had shocked her, and then when she and Iseabail had read the books, she'd started wondering if perhaps there could be more than just tender feelings between a man and a woman. The first of his two highly inappropriate letters had ignited her desire for *unparalleled bliss* and Joshua had nearly delivered it that night in her library, despite them having shared very little physical intimacy. That encounter had made her realize how much she had missed in her marriage bed.

Iseabail slowly lowered herself onto Phoebe's bed, her black bombazine gown of mourning a stark contrast to the pale-yellow bedding. "I can't believe you asked your solicitor to find those books. How did Forrester react to your request?"

"The first time he ignored me and continued shuffling papers."

Iseabail chuckled. "That hardly sounds like Forrester."

"I know. I voiced the request a second time, and I believe my cheeks may have turned to the shade of the ripest red apple you could imagine."

Iseabail's brow furrowed and she placed the damp cloth she always carried across her forehead as she laid back on the bed. It was a sign of the daily sickness Iseabail had felt since realizing she was pregnant. She carried the cloth with her everywhere. "Did he acknowledge your second request?"

It was a scene Phoebe had played over and over in her mind. "He jumped to his feet, gathered the contracts I had just signed for the new distribution of our spring hats and said, 'I will get on it right away, Lady Drake.' Then he rushed out the door without another word. I think I embarrassed him more than myself."

"Is it possible he felt something—else?"

"The man is a paragon of propriety." At least she'd believed him to be until his first letter. Then, their encounter in her library had shown just how wicked he could be. His latest letter...well, it was far from the correspondence of a paragon. It was gloriously unprincipled and she found she liked that side of him so much more.

"Except when it comes to you." Iseabail took a deep breath and exhaled.

"What is that supposed to mean?"

"When he first approaches you, he smiles as he bows. With everyone else, he gives a polite nod."

She shook her head in dismissal of the idea as she began running through past encounters with Forrester one at a time. "I hardly think a smile makes a man fall off his pedestal of propriety." Yet he did smile in her company, and then his second letter...and at the house party they truly had been *debauched, depraved and downright dirty*. She would take it one step further and describe them as filthy, debased, immoral—and she had never enjoyed herself more thoroughly.

She closed her eyes and confessed. "Last February at my house party he told Ross and Astley that he had been courting me for months."

Iseabail's mouth dropped open. "Why didn't you tell me he was courting you?"

"That's just it. If the man had been courting me, I was more ignorant to the event than you. To make matters worse, he said Nithesdale approved the match."

"So Nithesdale knew of his courtship, but you did not?"

"According to what Forrester said, yes."

"Has he kissed you?"

"Of course not." Lie number two.

"Has he taken you for a ride in the park?"

"He is my man of affairs. He manages my money, he handles the banks, and he handles any disputes I have at my business. I have considered him a friend and a confidant for years, but a suitor? Most certainly not."

Iseabail frowned. "Does his lower station bother you?"

"I haven't given it any thought." She found it preferable.

"You should. If you were to marry—"

"You're jumping too far, too fast. I haven't even considered him courting me," Phoebe insisted; but then looked down at the letter in her sleeve.

"Suppose he did want to court you, would his lower station be a concern?"

"No."

"You didn't give it much thought."

"That's because I have no wish to marry at all, let alone marry an aristocrat. My parents decided my first marriage for me. *If* I marry again, it will be my decision."

"I thought you loved your husband?"

Phoebe smiled. "I was very fond of Richard. The Countess of Astley introduced us because she knew I wanted someone who was kind. Richard treated me well, but it was never a love match despite our tender feelings. Yet I feel betrayed by the manner in which he did not disclose the state of our financial affairs. I know it was his male ego that kept him from telling his much younger wife that he'd made a hash of everything, but I still have a hard time forgiving him. My father was made a baron because of his business acumen, not because he was born into the peerage. He had viewed my marriage as a shrewd business move for growth in our family business. I trusted him to choose someone who understood business."

"What would women do if we weren't chattel to the men in our lives?"

Phoebe shrugged. "It made little difference to me. When my father was made baron, I suddenly became an *honourable*. I lost all my friends and found myself alone in a school full of girls born to the aristocracy. When it came time for my Season, it was not filled with friends or lords wanting to make my acquaintance. It was full of dowry hunters who viewed me as property to tolerate.

"When the countess introduced me to Richard, I was thrilled with the match. Richard was the only man of the ton who treated me like a queen, and when he offered for my hand, my father accepted. He said a match like Richard was beneficial to us all. I was too ignorant to know what questions a bride should ask, let alone question my betrothed's knowledge of business. Apparently, my father was as well."

"Since I never had a Season, I wouldn't know what one entailed. Yet still, I find myself a duchess. Do you want to give up the hopes of holding rank within the peerage?"

Phoebe sighed. "Since I find the ton tedious and bothersome, it hardly matters whom I marry."

"Then why do you do it?"

"Do what?"

"Why do you host scandalous house parties year after year for members of the ton?"

Why had she started hosting house parties with all the members of the ton who skirted the edge of polite society when she herself had never engaged in a tryst at any of them? "I was bored."

Iseabail laughed. "Bored?"

She sighed, long and deep. "When Richard died, I discovered he had left me everything ...and nothing at all."

"You must be joking." Iseabail knew exactly what she was speaking of. Her own father had done worse. He'd died and left his six young daughters destitute and knee-deep in scandal. The very reason why Iseabail had married the dying Duke of Nithesdale and was carrying her husband's heir. "What did you do?"

Phoebe's laugh was humorless and short as she sat down on the bed next to Iseabail. "Like most young women who find themselves in a scrape, I turned to my husband's family. His older brother, the earl, did not reply to my correspondence and Richard's younger brother would have helped, but he was as penniless as me. So, I turned to a man I knew could help."

Iseabail's brows drew together as if she knew exactly what happened. "Who?"

"Henry Jarvis. He was expressing interest in buying my family's business before Richard died."

Iseabail scowled. "That horrible man."

She nodded. "Initially, he was a welcome ally. I soon found out how wrong I was, and how despicable he could be."

Iseabail placed her hand on Phoebe's and squeezed. She smiled back at her, their bond of hatred for the despicable Henry Jarvis only strengthened their friendship.

"At the time I was devastated. I was twenty years old with no idea what to do. My parents were dead, my husband was dead, I had no money, and a man was expressing an interest I didn't want. I was desperate.

"It was Nithesdale who had the presence of mind to check on me." She shook her head, still in disbelief of Nithesdale's actions. "What man of the ton worries about his friend's widow? I was so grateful I nearly fell at his feet when he arrived at the house. I'd already let all the servants go, and I had no one. I was so desperate for any assistance I would have done anything he asked if he would just tell me what to do."

Iseabail stiffened and Phoebe immediately understood how her words may be misinterpreted.

"No dear. Unlike Mr. Jarvis, your husband was never that sort of man. He brought in Forrester, who was a couple years older than me and such a dashing figure. He was intelligent and held himself with a worldly air most men of twenty-three only dream of possessing. He was exactly the person I needed to make my family business profitable once more. After the first year, when he showed me the business accounts and the profits in my personal accounts that had grown month after month, I nearly fainted."

"I can imagine the relief you felt." Iseabail rubbed her stomach once more, changing the direction of the tiny little circles she appeared to draw with the palm of her hand.

"I hosted my first house party to let Jarvis know I had become a success without becoming his mistress. I stupidly wanted him to believe that I gave myself freely to other men, while I'd refused his offer of money."

"I would have done the same." Iseabail smiled. "But weren't you interested in Forrester?"

She shook her head. "He was everything that is professional. He never so much as hinted that he was interested in anything beyond assisting me as my man of affairs."

"I didn't ask if he expressed interest. I asked if you held a *tendre* for him?"

She blushed. "What young woman wouldn't look at Forrester and fantasize about those strong thighs?"

It was Iseabail's turn to blush as she laughed and bumped her shoulder against Phoebe's. "You truly were a wanton widow."

"A wanton widow perhaps in my mind, and to the gossip among the ton, but I'm only daring in my dreams."

Iseabail paused, her eyes going wide. "You mean you never—"

She shook her head. "Only with my husband."

"I can't believe it. I would have never guessed your husband was your only paramour." Iseabail's eyes went to the letter in her sleeve. "Does Forrester know?"

"I would hardly discuss such a topic with him, but I would imagine even he believes that I have lived a less than virtuous life since Richard passed."

"So, what does his letter say?"

Phoebe got up and walked across the room to look out the window. The ancient castle walls were surrounded by a moat deep enough for one to drown in and never be found. Perhaps she could just disappear and not answer Iseabail's questions. She sighed and turned toward her friend, still unable to confess the contents of the letter.

"I didn't tell you that Ross suggested Forrester and I become engaged."

Iseabail gasped. "Why would he suggest that?"

Despite every outrageous act she and Iseabail had allowed the ton to believe they had partaken in within the past few months, none of it had occurred. Well, *something* had occurred, but Phoebe had not been involved.

"To restore your reputation."

Iseabail scoffed. "That hardly signifies. The ton has branded me a bastard, and a title climbing whore since before I married Nithesdale. I am neither, but I can't prove it. What could they possibly say about me now that could be worse?"

Phoebe winced. She would have to tell Iseabail the current gossip. "They say that you and I are lovers, and the longer I stay at Caerlaverock, the worse the rumors will get."

Iseabail's hand went to her stomach once more, this time she looked as if she would cast up her accounts. "That does seem to be a bit more scandalous than I had bargained for."

"Exactly. It was one thing for people to believe the two of us were involved with Nithesdale, but for the ton to believe we continued on together after his death can only hurt you more."

"What about you?"

Phoebe smiled the sultry grin she had grown accustomed to giving the men of the ton. "It makes me the wanton widow I have always been."

Despite the obvious queasy state of her stomach, Iseabail

stood up and gave her best saucy tilt of her hip as she ran her hand down her side in the practiced move she'd perfected to win the heart of one man. "Then let them believe we are *two* wanton widows."

Phoebe laughed. "What happened to the inhibited woman I used to know?"

Iseabail sobered. "Life dealt me blows that threatened to break me, but I refused to let them."

"I'm sorry. I didn't mean to—"

"Stop." Iseabail walked over and put her arm around Phoebe. "I know what you're doing."

"What am I doing?" It was no use. Iseabail would not let it go until she knew exactly what was in the letter.

"You're avoiding the question."

"What question?"

"Don't be coy with me, Lady Phoebe Drake." She scolded her like a mother of six, not a first-time mother of one in the womb. "What's in the letter?"

"You won't like it."

"I may love it."

"You won't."

"Phoebe, let me be the judge."

She bit her lip and then let the words spew from her mouth so quickly she wasn't certain she said everything she should. "Forrester has been keeping tabs on the Duke of Ross since we left the house party, and as it turns out, he's on his way here to claim you." She winced, waiting for the words to sink in.

Iseabail's arm slipped from around her shoulders and she wanted to pull her back and give her the comfort she needed.

"I can't let him do that."

"I know."

"It would be wrong," she whispered as if saying it alone was a sin.

"Would it?"

Iseabail turned to her, conviction ringing in her voice. "Of course it would. I made a promise to Nithesdale."

"Nithesdale is dead. What about you? You care for Ross."

"No. I'm carrying my husband's heir and I will not allow society's gossip to destroy my baby's future."

"What about Ross?"

She laughed, the sound humorless and bitter. "The Duke of Ross will forget about me in a month. Let him come, but he will be turned away at the gates." Iseabail swept out of the room in a flurry of silks and satin, the letter completely forgotten.

Phoebe walked over to the fire and pulled out the letter from her sleeve. She may have shared some of the content of Joshua's letter, but she did not confess all of it. She read the letter for the thousandth time in the past few hours and fantasized about all the delectable things Joshua Forrester offered to do. She had been bold when requesting the books of unparalleled *sin* because her cousin had needed the information she couldn't provide. As a widow who was purported to be the mistress of a duke, one would believe her to be knowledgeable in all manner of debauchery.

Except she wasn't.

She had been a widow much longer than she'd been married, and her husband had not been one to inspire *bliss*. She read Joshua's letter once more, slowly taking in each word in the beautiful scrolling script of Forrester's strong hand.

"Ross is coming for the duchess, and my dear Lady, I am coming for you. I have spent years waiting for you and I will not give up on us now when we are so close to the unparalleled bliss I promised."

"I'm sorry, Joshua, but *bliss* is not worth the price of my freedom." She hoped he heard her words, otherwise she would have to run... Or throw another house party and create a scandal no gentleman could ignore, even one of no rank.

Two

Dear Mr. Forrester,

I appreciate your offer in your latest correspondence; however, I must decline your invitation. The duchess has had a rather difficult pregnancy and I believe it to be in her best interest, and the baby's, that I remain at Caerlaverock throughout her confinement. We would both be grateful if you could dispel the rumors of the two of us holding a tendre for one another. I am simply a female relative assisting the duchess through her sorrow and confinement. Please advise Ross he will not be allowed entry into Caerlaverock. The duchess is determined to protect her child at any cost and has banned all men from entering the castle walls. This is to include you and all male staff.

The footmen are being temporarily housed at the dowager house outside the walls of Caerlaverock.

Paddington, Her Grace's ever-faithful butler, will be the only man allowed entry into the estate. If you need to communicate with Her Grace, you may do so in writing, or I will meet you at the dowager house and bring any papers she may need to read or sign to her.

Please understand this is a happy, but also sad and stressful time in the duchess's life. The midwife, along with the duchess and myself, believe this to be the best course of action for Her Grace's health and the babe's.

With kindest regards,
Lady Drake

—A letter written at the end of April 1811 to Mr. Joshua Forrester, Esquire from Lady Phoebe Drake citing an article in The Whispers of the Ton gossip rag which accused the duchess of attempting to seduce male staff to become impregnated with a bastard child and claim it as the late Duke of Nithesdale's heir. In truth, it was to dissuade Ross and Mr. Forrester from traveling to Caerlaverock.

December 1811

She was here. Somewhere inside the cold, damp stone walls of Caerlaverock Castle, Lady Phoebe Drake was doing what she did best. Hiding from him.

Joshua, solicitor to the Duchess of Nithesdale, and the lady in hiding, sat in the blue drawing room of the ancient castle where he had served the former Duke of Nithesdale prior to his passing. The same drawing room where he had introduced the duchess to Lady Phoebe Drake almost nine years earlier. So many firsts had occurred for him in this room. His first ducal client had hired him here after summoning him to the Scottish Lowlands.

"Mr. Forrester."

The duchess walked into the room, or rather waddled into the room, if he was being completely honest. Her gait was much different in the late stages of pregnancy than what it had been the last time he'd seen her. It took everything in him to school his utter shock at how large she had become. Her attire looked more like a bombazine tent than a gown. Just the fact that his mind went in that direction made him wince from the mental slap his mother was giving him from heaven. *Apologies, Mamma.*

He rose to his feet and bowed. "Your Grace, I didn't expect to see you. I had meant to meet with Lady Drake regarding a rather important matter. I did not mean to undermine your directive that no men enter the castle during your confinement. I understand why you would like to avoid any hint of scandal that may bring into question the parentage of your child."

The duchess rolled her eyes. "Please stop calling me 'Your Grace.' And secondly, you asked to see Lady Drake, not me. I can hardly decline your admittance to Caerlaverock when you're not here to see me. Besides, you could hardly impregnate me now."

"I will never forget your station, Your Grace. That is why I'm surprised you're the one greeting me, and not Lady

Drake." He hoped that was enough to cover his shock at seeing the duchess in her current condition. The duchess he had served pre-pregnancy looked nothing like the woman before him now.

"I will sack you, if you don't start speaking less formally, and gawking at my protruding belly."

His eyes shot to hers, heat rising up his neck. He hadn't even realized he was staring at her stomach. "Of course, Your Grace."

The duchess laughed but her mirth quickly turned into a sharp gasp as she froze in front of the settee. Joshua quickly moved to her side and grabbed her arm to steady her. "Are you alright, Your Grace?"

The duchess took a deep breath and exhaled slowly, then smiled. "My child is attempting to murder me. Slowly."

"Would you like me to send for the doctor or midwife?" Dear Lord, don't let her go into labor while he was there.

She shook her head and gave a feeble smile. "I'm told false labor is to be expected. If I sit for a bit, everything will be fine."

Joshua nodded and helped her lower herself to the settee. Once she was seated, she gave another sigh and waved him over to the seat across from her. "To what do we owe the pleasure of this unexpected visit today? I thought you were coming after the first of the year to discuss the title and its holdings."

"Are you worried about the holdings being passed on to your child?"

The duchess shook her head and rubbed her stomach.

"I'm not concerned. I know this little demon inside me is a boy, and I have nothing to worry about."

Joshua refrained from wincing. "But if it's a girl?"

"Then my daughter will always have a home at Caerlaverock and I have faith in you to ensure the rest of the ducal estates, tenants, and servants are well taken care of."

With that statement he did wince. "Mr. Jarvis has made it blatantly clear that my services will no longer be needed if he is the duke's heir."

She leaned as far forward as her stomach would allow and patted his hand. "Then you have nothing to worry about, because I know this child is a boy. A girl would never treat her mother in such a roughshod manner."

He nodded his agreement but wasn't certain a mother could determine if she was having a boy or a girl with that sort of barometer. If the duchess had a girl, it would not bode well for the servants or tenants of estates. "I'm actually here to see Lady Drake."

The duchess grinned. Her expression somehow slier than the cat who ate the proverbial creme. "As you said. You don't need to hide your affection for Phoebe from me. I couldn't be happier for the two of you."

He cleared his throat and nearly choked. "I—I assure you I don't know what you mean."

"Mr. Forrester, how long have I known you?"

"I've been in your service for almost a year, Your Grace."

She waved her hand in dismissal of the meager timeframe. "I have known you since I was fourteen years old. I am now three and twenty."

She spoke as if she were ready to move to the dowager house. "Our relationship when you were a child was a bit different than what it is now."

"That's true. You used to be my knight in shining armor."

He blinked. Surely the duchess did not mean what he thought she meant, and yet for the life of him, he didn't know how to respond. If Phoebe had been sitting in front of him, saying the same thing, the flirtation would have been automatic. "I hardly know what to say."

The duchess stretched her back, appearing more uncomfortable by the moment. "You don't have to say anything. What I'm trying to convey to you is that I am aware of the attraction between the two of you. How I missed it before is beyond comprehension. I've spent a good part of these past few months running over the different times I've witnessed the two of you together over the years, and the attraction was rather obvious. Yet not one person seemed to be aware of it. Except of course, Nithesdale."

"He was the most observant man I've ever known. Nothing got past him."

Her eyes teared up. "I miss him every day and I wish he was going to be here to see his son born."

"I suspect he is still plotting and moving us on his chessboard from heaven."

She chuckled. "I believe you are correct."

Phoebe walked into the room and her eyes went wide as she froze just inside the door. He had believed she was avoiding him, her stunned expression proved otherwise.

She'd been unaware of his arrival. He glanced at the duchess, who wore a pleased expression on her face, and he realized he had an ally where he had least expected. His gaze returned to Phoebe as he drank in her beauty and rose to his feet.

"Forgive me. I didn't mean to interrupt," she said and began to back out of the room, her gaze landing everywhere but on him.

"Don't be ridiculous." The duchess let out a deep breath as she finished speaking. The girth of her stomach taking a tremendous toll on her decorum.

Joshua crossed the room, unable to stop his perusal of Phoebe's lush curves immaculately displayed in an emerald green day dress with pearl beading across her breasts. He bowed before her, suddenly envisioning her being round with pregnancy. The idea held more appeal than he'd ever imagined.

Phoebe pregnant with their child.

He took her hand and kissed the back of her knuckles, allowing his lips to linger as he looked up into her eyes and conveyed exactly what he would like to do to her without saying a word.

Color rushed to her cheeks and before she could pull away, he placed her hand on his forearm, unable to take his eyes off her as he escorted her to the chair next to his. God, how he'd missed her. Her exile within the walls of Caerlaverock had been killing him. To see her again was like breathing the country air after being trapped in London for an entire year. The weight on his chest eased.

Despite being drawn to where she bit her lip, he didn't

miss the surreptitious tuck of her other hand into the folds of her skirt. She'd walked into the library with a folded piece of paper that she was currently attempting to hide from his view.

The duchess was a woman on a mission, however, and called Phoebe out. "Is that your New Year's Resolution list?"

Phoebe reddened. "I'll show you later."

"Nonsense. Read it to me now."

"Out loud?" she squeaked.

"Well, of course. That's half the fun." The duchess addressed him as he sat down next to Phoebe, his leg brushing the skirts of her gown. "Phoebe has never made a New Year's Resolution List. Have you, Mr. Forrester?"

"Not a list, per se, but as a child my parents instructed us to write down one resolution each year. Then on New Year's Day, we pledged to keep it."

The duchesses grinned. "See, Phoebe? It's a marvelous tradition. You have years of pledges to make up for." She turned to him. "I told her she must have some child-like intentions and some adult resolutions to cover the years she missed."

He nodded and found himself vastly interested as to what she would write for her childhood and adulthood pledges. Would any be scandalous?

Phoebe cleared her throat. "Yes, well, it's not complete yet."

"How many have you completed?"

"Six... I mean five." Her gaze darted to him and then back to the duchess.

"Only five? I see we have some work to do. Tell us what your first five are."

Phoebe acted as if the duchess had asked her to undress on the spot. A thought he found very appealing. Phoebe was horrified.

"They're actually very silly. I'll just burn it," she said as she rose to walk over to the fireplace. Without thinking, Joshua snatched the list from her hand.

"Joshua!" she exclaimed and lunged for the piece of foolscap, but Joshua was prepared; he did have a younger sister he used to love to torment. He grinned and rose to his feet to hold it out of her reach. Phoebe jumped and fell against his chest. He steadied her with his free hand, pulling her tightly against the length of his body, and she looked up into his eyes. He had no doubt the raw need he was experiencing was smoldering in the dark depths of his gaze. Her breath hitched and for a moment, he thought about kissing her.

Until sanity overruled his baser needs and he released her. He looked away as he dropped his hand from her waist and stepped back. The loss of her touch devastating to his senses. It was as if he lost a part of himself he'd only ever experienced with her.

Phoebe immediately turned away and the two of them looked up to find the duchess watching them in amazed silence. Her Grace was the first to recover.

"*Mr. Forrester.*" The duchess's formal address brought attention to Phoebe's slip of tongue with his Christian name, and her color deepened. "Since Lady Drake is reluctant to read her list aloud, perhaps you could read it for her."

Joshua couldn't stop the small grin from forming on his lips. It was the next best thing to holding her in his arms. To learn Phoebe's secret pledges was a gift in and of itself. She'd held her emotions tight to her chest for as long as he had known her. He lifted the paper and read the first line.

"'Number one. Build a...'" His breath escaped him. The words jumbled and he blinked several times as a lump formed in his throat. He couldn't speak. Couldn't look at her. He wanted to with every fiber in his being, but to gaze upon Phoebe now, after reading those words written in her own delicate handwriting, would be the death of him. He had to breathe. There was no way a man could read that word written in her hand and not grow instantly hard. "'Build a snowman.'" The words came out like a moan.

"Well, that is easy enough to fulfill. There are several inches of fresh snow on the ground as we speak, with more falling by the moment. I would suggest you alter your pledge just a bit, however, and build a snow woman," the duchess interjected. "My sisters and I refused to build a snowman when I was growing up. It started when Ailsa was five. She asked our parents how a snowman could be born without a mamma. From that day forward, we only made snow women."

He had no doubt Phoebe would have loved that story, if she wasn't desperately trying to think of a way to extract the list from his hands. He'd be damned if he'd give it up now after the salacious taste of her innermost desires he'd read so far.

"What's next, Mr. Forrester?" Her Grace asked.

This was heaven and hell. His mind stumbled on every word Phoebe had written. His body wanted to act. The duchess was only making it worse, and exponentially better, by forcing Phoebe to share her desires—with him. "'Have a snowball fight and...' You've never..." His brain faltered for an appropriate way to phrase the question. "You've never held a snowball in your hand and licked it?" he asked.

Phoebe's cheeks flamed in the most adorable fashion as she shook her head. Who would have thought he would enjoy reading her resolution list so much.

"Lick it?" the duchess asked.

He was definitely going to hell, but damn if the place hadn't become appealing in the last few minutes.

"What he means is *eat* it. I've never eaten snow."

His mouth quirked as her gaze glanced off him and landed back in her lap. Oh, but this would be rather enjoyable if he could keep his body in check. He moved on to the next item on her list.

"'Number three,'" he continued. "'Make...'" His throat seized.

"Yes? What does she want to make? A new hat? Holiday biscuits? What?" the duchess inquired.

He stretched his neck in an effort to swallow the lump that went down like a dry piece of flaming bark from the hearth. "'Make...'" He coughed, not certain he wouldn't die in the suffocating heat of the roaring fire.

"Are you ill, Mr. Forrester?" the duchess asked as she started to get up, but he motioned for her to stay seated. Phoebe did the opposite of attempting to assist him. She sat down on the settee and clasped her hands together in an attempt to hide the tremor he observed traveling throughout her body.

"I'm fine," he croaked. "I just swallowed wrong."

"Let me pour you some tea," the duchess suggested.

He held up his hand once more. "No, that's not necessary. I'm quite alright," he replied with a scratchy voice that sounded as if he had indeed swallowed the piece of wood. For Phoebe's sake, he would make it through her list if it was the last thing he did.

Damn, what a glorious death that would be.

"'Make a snow angel.'" Joshua gasped out her third wish as he schooled his expression before asking, "I understand some feel the need to call out to the Lord while experiencing the bliss of the moment. Can you imagine?" He most certainly was, and he was losing the battle with his trousers at the moment. They were growing quite uncomfortable.

Her response was short and to the point. "No." Smart woman. Less was more at this point.

"'Four, go sledding.'" His mind strayed to the manner in which she wanted to ride the sled. Holy hell. Her list was ensuring he qualified for sainthood by continuing to read it without giving anything away. Well, almost anything. He moved to stand behind the pianoforte to keep his hard cock hidden from view.

"Five, go on a sleigh ride."

She licked her lips as if her mouth had grown as parched as his. He wanted that sleigh ride most of all. To see her in such a manner. Dear God.

He had dreamed of it so many times over the years.

"Oh, that sounds marvelous, Phoebe."

"Marvelous," he echoed.

"Mr. Forrester, you will have to help her complete her list. I'm afraid I won't be able to do much with this child making me as big as a castle."

He couldn't take his eyes off Phoebe. "It would be my pleasure."

"You are not that big, Iseabail," Phoebe insisted.

You cannot hide from me anymore, Phoebe. "You have one more item on your list," he interjected.

"You do have six!" the duchess exclaimed with so much glee—one would think it was her list of sexual endeavors.

"'Go for a carriage ride,'" Joshua read and stopped there. To read further would display the worst of decorum. His lips, however, devoured the words as he silently absorbed the full implications of her sixth resolution—a yearning he could not stop painted the erotic fantasies in his mind. This was torture.

"What is it?" the duchess asked.

Startled, he glanced up. "What?"

"Number six on her list. Go for a carriage ride and what?"

"I...I... Nothing. It stops at a carriage ride," he lied as he did everything in his power to keep his body from betraying just exactly what Phoebe wanted to accomplish.

"But I saw your lips moving as if you were reading it to yourself," Her Grace pressed. She truly was learning the stubborn insistent manner of the ton. As if it were God's decree they be dogmatic. It would drive the duke mad if he were here, yet Joshua couldn't deny her persistence was the perfect demeanor for a duchess.

He stared at the list, unable to think of a lie.

Phoebe grabbed it from his hand, the edge of the paper tearing slightly. He hadn't even realized she'd risen from her seat and approached him, he'd been too lost in her list.

She flashed the piece of foolscap in the direction of the duchess. "It was my doodling at the bottom of the paper that distracted him. See?" She quickly folded it in half and then in half once more before tucking it into the ribbon under her ample breasts.

Breasts he wanted to get lost in... His gaze shot to hers but she immediately turned to look out the window, avoiding him as she bit her lip in the most seductive manner. Did she know what she was doing to him?

"Well, that's rather anticlimactic."

She had no idea. His body throbbed with the need to spend.

The duchess sighed, then clapped her hands together, causing him and Phoebe to jump as one. Her Grace grinned. "I insist you start on the list immediately so that Phoebe can finish her childhood resolutions before the new year."

That was the best idea he'd ever heard.

Phoebe's eyes nearly popped out of her head as she

backed away from him. "Don't be silly. Mr. Forrester didn't travel all this way to go out and play in the snow."

He cleared his throat. "On the contrary, there's nothing I would rather do than to cross off the items on your list...with you." *Every last lewd and lascivious desire you imagined and put on your list for me to complete.*

Her face heated. "It's not necessary."

"On the contrary, it's essential," he said.

"I agree. I may not be able to enjoy the winter season in my current condition, but I can certainly ensure you take your pleasure," the duchess declared.

Over and over and over again.

The duchess struggled to her feet and tugged on the servant's bell pull. When the butler entered the room, Phoebe's objections died. "Paddington, Lady Drake and Mr. Forrester will need their coats as well as mittens and mufflers. They will need a sled and have the sleigh brought around from the stables."

"Your Grace, it's really not necessary. It was a fantastical list, not a *real* one." There was a sparkle in Phoebe's eyes as if, despite her protestations, she wanted to complete her list as much as he did.

He swore to make a reality. "I vow that we will complete every last item on your list."

The duchess beamed. "Oh, this is so exciting," she said as she traced small circles across her protruding stomach. Her new habit was fascinating, yet somewhat disconcerting. "Phoebe, you can try that new bonnet you've been working on for winter country attire to keep a lady's head warm."

He should stop this endeavor. He'd come here with a specific purpose in mind, but not only was the duchess excited for her best friend, Phoebe was beginning to light up with the possibility of playing in the snow.

And more.

It was as if she had been denied the simple pleasures that should be natural for a child, and for an adult. He suspected her list had initially contained activities she had wished to experience in her youth, but then she'd added a second part to each wish—the romantic hopes of a young woman entering marriage. Those fantasies were just as tragically unaccomplished as the dreams of her adolescence. It was this sudden realization that made him decide to delay the grievous business with the Countess of Astley for one more day.

It was time he satisfied a New Year's resolution of his own.

Three

Dear Cousin,

It is with humble regret I write this letter. The Earl of Astley has been seized by the French on our voyage from The United States to Spain. Due to the war between our countries, I was hesitant to notify your war office lest I further the conflict and cause an international incident, or Britain revoke my license to conduct business with Spain, Portugal and Canada. My license was the very reason why I was comfortable transporting the earl to Spain. I did not, however, ~~*know of his espionage*~~ *expect to be fired upon by the French because the earl was aboard my ship.*

My ship, the Fairhaven, suffered damage to the mainsail during a ~~*bloody battle*~~ *"misunderstanding" with the French Navy in* ~~*the Bay of Biscay*~~ *open sea and was* ~~*taken by force*~~ *peacefully boarded. French Navy*

Captain Rochefort informed me he was there to seize Astley and no one else. Captain Rochefort threatened to ~~burn my ship~~ seize my ship with everyone on board unless I turned Astley over to the French Navy. Astley stepped forward and surrendered himself. ~~The damned fool~~.

It is unclear how the French knew Astley was on ~~a mission for the Crown~~ my schooner. If the person responsible for the heinous act of reporting to the French is one of my crew, I will charge him with mutiny. The French captain has ~~rightly~~ ridiculously accused Astley of spying and said Bonaparte would decide how much ~~blood money~~ ransom would be a reasonable amount for the return of a member of the Crown's peerage who was in the service of his King. They have recovered a ~~damning~~ personal letter written by Astley to his ~~non-existent wife~~ family as evidence of his perfidy.

I would deliver the dire news myself, but I cannot risk my crew being impressed into the British Navy. Prior to his capture, Astley stated his family always retires to the earl's estate in ~~the bloody wilds of~~ Scotland for the holidays. As I am currently ~~bollocks~~ deep in negotiations with the French to obtain ~~the bloody fool's~~ Astley's release prior to the holidays, I would be indebted to you if you could deliver the ~~devastating~~ news to his mother. I don't know if you are acquainted with the Countess of Astley, but I made a promise to the earl that his mother would know the truth of his fate. I feel this type of news should be delivered in person, not by correspondence that may or may not reach Astley's family.

Please convey my deepest regret for the ~~clusterfuck~~
debacle.

> *God's speed,*
> *Miles*

> *—A redacted letter to Joshua Forrester, Esquire,*
> *London, England from his cousin, American Captain*
> *Miles Gallagher of the Fairhaven merchant ship, in*
> *reference to the capture of Simon Clark, Earl of Astley,*
> *November 1811. The final letter did not disclose Astley's*
> *crimes against the French.*

He was waiting for her in the great hall. Looking down the main staircase, she could see Joshua pacing back and forth across the ancient stone as if he were one of the conquering leaders of the English army that had invaded this castle time and time again. Would he burn it down if she refused to join him? Storm the stairs if she did not descend?

She watched him from the shadows, his dark hair glistening in the light from the chandelier. He was like no other man she'd ever known. When Nithesdale had first introduced him to her, she'd had no use for attractive men. To be honest, she had no use for any man other than Nithesdale, who'd been more of a father to her than her own had been. Joshua had merely been a brilliant advisor. Nothing more.

Yet he'd slowly snuck into her psyche and had begun to mean more. She began to anticipate his arrival for their business meetings like a young woman looking forward to meeting her beau at a ball. Then their meetings had become scandalously more intimate, often occurring over a meal, or late into the evening on her request. When time had escaped them, Joshua had slept in one of the guest rooms. Down the opposite hall from her bed chamber, too far away to tempt her into acting inappropriately. Like he was now.

Already wearing his greatcoat, he held her coat over his arm as if he would assist her in dressing. She wanted him to do the opposite. He wanted the opposite as well. It had been blatantly apparent as he'd secretly consumed her words on the list. She'd noticed the instant his trousers had become uncomfortable and he'd attempted to hide behind the pianoforte.

Her own body had prepared for him instantaneously, growing heated and wet. So wet.

His tall, athletic build was divine. He sported lean muscle and sinew, without the assistance of padding or corsets so many men of the ton wore. Joshua didn't require anything to mold his body, it came to him naturally and she'd been hard pressed to determine where he'd acquired such masculine grace. A man who worked behind a desk all day should not possess such raw virility.

She bit the inside of her lower lip, then closed her eyes and willed her heartbeat to slow. It would do her no good to fall down the stairs at his feet. Rolling her shoulders once to release the tension, she opened her eyes and headed down the stairs with what she hoped was a look of pleased serenity.

She watched as he turned and matched her step for step.

With a longer, stronger, purposeful stride he met her at the bottom of the staircase while never taking his eyes from hers. She stopped one step from the bottom, her breath coming faster as she realized he was still taller. Then he bowed over her hand and kissed the back of her knuckles hidden by her gloves. How she wished her skin was bare so that she might feel the touch of his lips on her skin once more.

His gaze strayed to the wool bonnet she had designed specifically for ladies who traveled to Scotland. Through the years she had avoided visiting Caerlaverock during the winter months because of the frigid weather. This year, however, she'd made up her mind to stay with Iseabail through the bitter cold months and necessity had driven her to design something warmer.

Her current wool bonnet might appear less ornate upon one's initial sighting, but closer inspection displayed delicate embroidered Scottish heather with beadwork along the brim. She had been very pleased with the outcome, but was unsure of the reaction it would receive by members of the ton. She waited for Joshua's evaluation.

"You have far exceeded my expectations of what a Scottish bonnet should look like. It's quite beautiful, although the beauty of the woman wearing it may be influencing my opinion."

Her cheeks heated at the compliment. "Thank you, Mr. Forrester." He had always been kind with his remarks, but discussing her appearance was new.

He leaned in close, a twinkle in his eyes. "I believe we are beyond addressing each other so formally, don't you?"

She could not stop the blush from rising to her cheeks as his eyes traveled to her lips. She didn't know what to say, so she just nodded as he assisted her down the final step.

"I'm curious why you didn't make your bonnet out of beaver skin. Don't you think it would be more suitable to Scottish weather?"

"I've never understood a man's desire to wear a dead animal on his head, and I believe most women of the ton would share my opinion." She didn't say if every woman was escorted by a man who had his masculine appeal, they would be fainting within moments of donning a hat such as that.

He looked down at the beaver skin hat in his hand. "Does it offend you?"

"You are at the height of fashion and fashion never offends me. Just don't ask me to wear it." He tilted his head in deference to her comment and then assisted her into her winter redingote.

Their old comfortable camaraderie returning, she felt a surge of relief, until he asked his next question.

"Phoebe." The deep timbre of his voice sent tingles down her spine as he whispered her Christian name. "Are you ready to mark off the items on your list?"

She gave him an overly bright smile as if all she thought about was the fun in the snow Iseabail had spoken of. "I cannot wait. What shall we do first? Build a snow woman, have a snowball fight, or create snow angels?"

The corner of his mouth twitched before he said, "I took the liberty of having Mrs. Hagerty pack a picnic basket so that we might make an afternoon of it. First, we will take a sleigh ride to the top of the rise, and then sled down a nearby hill. After lunching, we can build a snow woman, make snow angels and then you can lick those snowballs you wrote about."

She nearly tripped on the deep rumble of his voice as he said "*lick*." The picture all too vivid in her mind. She cleared her throat. "That's not necessary."

"I mean to cross off *every* last item on your list."

"Oh." She tried not to let her nerves show, but she had planned it all out in her head so they would always be within sight of someone on the estate. It was the only way to keep herself from touching the man inappropriately. He, however, had made plans for the privacy her list required.

And he planned to complete the list. That scandalous, erotic list she had never in her wildest dreams expected to experience.

"If you would rather not go out..." He showed no emotion at all and she suddenly couldn't tell if he was anxiously awaiting her to say, *let's go partake in the debauchery you wrote about,* or if he would rather stay close to the castle so he could get this tedious task of performing the childish part of her list over with. For all she knew, since his last correspondence, he decided to hell with waiting for her, and he'd found himself a mistress to share his own depravity.

What if the nervous energy she'd thought she'd witnessed in Joshua before coming below stairs was actually dread? Oh, Lord. He'd probably moved on and forgotten all about their time together at the house party. While she had longed to experience the licentious intimacy she'd never shared with her husband, Joshua may have already experienced it with someone else. She should feel guilty or perhaps disloyal to the memory of Richard, but she did not. She had not chosen to marry him, but she had cared for him deeply, and she had been loyal to a man she hadn't loved throughout her marriage and for ten years after his death. Ten long years of solitary existence and her body was now hers to explore. To give to whom she desired, and today, Joshua was that man—if he so wished to be.

She seized the opportunity. "Yes, I would love to begin with a sleigh ride."

That devilish grin appeared on his lips and she almost changed her mind, but the chance to experience some of the freedoms she'd heard other women speak of was too great to pass up. He bowed slightly and then placed his hat on his head.

"Then let us be off," he said as he wrapped her arm around his forearm in a much too intimate manner. Her breath hitched, but she held her head high as they approached the door.

"I almost forgot," Joshua said as he stopped in front of the massive hewn doors adorned with heavy iron fixtures and framed with an array of blind arcades. He turned her back toward the door, capturing her gaze and refusing to release it as he stepped in and rested his forearm against the door above her head. Her heart tripped despite her feet being firmly planted on solid stone.

"Since I am usually working over the holidays, I have not

made a resolution in years. This year, however, I am inclined to make one," he said, his tone devilishly husky.

Realization struck her. From as far back as she could remember, Joshua had spent his holidays with her—working. Since that very first year when she'd lost her parents and her husband, he had filled her empty days with purpose.

His finger lifted her chin so that she had to meet his gaze. "Don't, Phoebe."

"Don't what? Feel guilty for taking you away from having a personal life throughout the holidays for the last ten years? For not letting you experience a tradition you held throughout your childhood?"

"I was with the woman I love on every one of those holidays."

"Don't be ridiculous. You were with *me*."

He didn't move. Nor did he deny where he'd been the past ten New Years. It was her turn to search his face for something. A lie? A jest? No, what she found was the truth in the depths of his deep brown eyes. He had spent his holidays with her because...because he *loved* her.

"And after spending so many holidays with you, dreaming of you, wishing I could hold you in my arms just once, this year I plan to fulfill my New Year's Resolution early. With your permission, of course."

Her heart was thundering. "Very well."

"May I kiss you, Phoebe?"

"Yes." It was the least she could do.

She wasn't even certain she had vocalized her assent before

he closed the distance between them, his gaze holding every wish he'd guarded for the past ten years. Ten Years. She had been oblivious to the yearning of this man's heart for nearly ten years.

She moistened her lip, drawing his gaze to where she ran the tip of her tongue in invitation. Joshua bent down, his angular, hard length folding more than what could possibly be comfortable. She closed her eyes as his warm lips touched hers in a soft and sensual exploration. His hand grazed her rib cage, resting below her breast. Desire unfurled throughout her body and her need to touch him overruled every one of her inhibitions.

Until he pulled away, ending the most tender and giving kiss she had ever experienced. It hadn't been like their embrace in her library, that had been raw and consuming. This kiss had given her a taste of his heart and how it beat for her. Only her.

She blinked as he tucked something in his inside jacket pocket. "I needed the list so that I ensure we fulfill every last item you desire."

Her hand flew to where she had tucked her naughty resolutions.

Blast. "You tricked me."

"I am a lawyer who has his client's best interests at heart."

Phoebe buttoned her coat, but knew she must set the ground rules for whatever was happening between them. "I don't want to hurt you; you are the last person on earth I want to hurt. You mean too much to me, but you must know that I will not marry you."

His expression grew guarded. "Because I am in your employ?"

"Because I will never marry again. I can't."

He gave a thoughtful nod before wrapping her arm in his and turning toward the door. "I understand your reservations, but today, we have a list to conquer."

Damnation. She'd mucked things up with that list. She'd written it to cheer Iseabail, and give them a naughty giggle.

It had been a joke...but this man was no joke, and now her list was real. He was real, and daunting, and everything she would have wished for in a husband. She might have succumbed if she had still been a naive seventeen-year-old girl who didn't know marriage could steal everything from a woman including her dowry, the riches of her family business, and the security her parents had blindly entrusted to a gentleman who had a good heart and no business acumen whatsoever.

But her own personal experience had subjected her to a rude awakening no woman should experience. Her future had been stolen; turned over to her husband because of his standing in society and his sex, nothing more.

She couldn't let that happen again.

Yet this was Joshua. The man who had guided her from certain poverty back into prosperity while allowing her to hold the reins. He'd counseled her, but in the end the decisions had been solely hers to make. Never once had he attempted to snag hold and drive her curricle. He was not Richard, who had left her in the dark, oblivious to every financial misstep he had taken. If she knew one thing about men, she knew they were not created equal.

And *he* wanted to make her list a reality. Richard would have blushed and thrown her list in the fire, never to be spoken of again.

Joshua smiled, his gaze never leaving hers as he watched her reaction. "I have never had the privilege of being kissed in a castle, and I can honestly say there has only been one lady whom I've wanted to kiss in such a place. Kissing you in Caerlaverock Castle would be a boon for any man. For me, it is a fantasy come true."

Before she could change her mind on the entire after-noon, he stepped back and took her arm once more. They exited the castle without another word exchanged between them and approached the iron gate. Since Iseabail's preg-nancy, the castle gates had remained drawn with the footmen standing guard outside the gate and it had seemed like another prison wall barring her from life ever since they'd arrived at Caerlaverock for Iseabail's confinement period. The duchess had been as protective of her unborn babe as if it were the next regent.

The guards opened the gate to a winter wonderland that covered the landscape, and a gorgeous red sleigh adorned with plush crimson cushions and gold trim awaited them. The ducal crest was emblazoned on the side, and a groom held the reins to a single bay horse that snorted and shook its black mane as they approached.

"Would you like to pet him?"

"Pet him?" Her mind raced to exactly what she wanted to pet, and it had nothing to do with a horse.

Joshua's cheek twitched as if he knew exactly what she was thinking. "The horse. He's very gentle."

"He's massive." Her eyes strayed down the length of Joshua's body, and he swore under his breath.

"He is at your command, and will do whatever you wish." The look on his face told her exactly what he wished to do, causing the heat of anticipation to flow through her body.

Joshua escorted her over to the horse, took the reins from the groom, and held his hand out for the animal to sniff before he gently stroked the beast on the nose. He whispered softly in its ear, and as if it understood, the horse whinnied in response.

"His Royal Highness said he won't hurt you," Joshua confided.

"His Royal Highness?"

"Haven't you learned the names the Blair sisters give their horses?"

"I know there's a pony named Prinny."

"Yes, but he's not the only member of the royal family. His Royal Highness outranks Prinny, at least in the stable."

"Couldn't that be considered treason to mock our Regent with two horses named after him in such a fashion?"

His brow crinkled in mock severity. "I believe the Blair sisters proclaimed their stable honours the royal family."

"But will the Prince Regent see it as such?"

"Hopefully the names of the Blair sisters' horses in the Scottish Lowlands will never be of interest to him. Otherwise, we will have to rely on his understanding of childhood games."

Her grin slipped and Joshua stared at her as if he were trying to see into her years in the nursery, an experience she had not shared with anyone.

"What is it?" he asked.

She knew how to pretend many things, but lying to Joshua was not something she did well. "I was just wondering what it would be like to have such frivolity as a child."

"Well today is the day we change that." Joshua took her hand and gently pulled her towards His Royal Highness.

With his strong, firm grip around her wrist, Phoebe reached out and allowed the horse to sniff her palm. His Royal Highness took two deep breaths and then suddenly expelled a quick, warm, moist breath over her glove. She jumped and felt Joshua close the distance between their bodies as the horse drew back its head.

"Easy, His Royal Highness," Joshua soothed as the warmth of his body moved to touch the back of hers, and the motion had the opposite effect on her. Her breath caught as his hand came around her waist and pulled her back against his front. His fingers splayed across her stomach and she nearly moaned with the pleasure of every part of his body touching hers. His scent heightened her desire as her head fell back against his chest and his body engulfed hers. Even through the barrier of their clothing, the experience was intoxicating.

The horse calmed. Her hand shook and Joshua's lips brushed her neck as he ducked down below the brim of her bonnet and whispered in her ear, "He won't hurt you, trust me."

That was the problem. She did trust him. She didn't trust herself. It would be too easy to fall into this man's arms and lose herself to the passion. The security. And then everything she had worked so hard to earn would be his. Not hers. His. Just like it had been with Richard.

She pulled away and stumbled. The horse yanked its head back and Phoebe strode toward the sleigh where she rigidly awaited Joshua to assist her up. He talked to His Royal Highness a bit longer and then strolled to her side, not once giving any indication that her abrupt departure dissuaded him from his goals.

He lifted her into the seat and asked, "Would you like to drive?"

"Me? I've never driven a conveyance in my life. I've never even ridden on a horse."

"Truly? Not even as a young girl?"

"Never. I was learning how to become a lady."

"But ladies ride all the time."

"My mother did not want my complexion to break out in more spots." It had become second nature to protect her nose from the outdoors. Her mother had cursed her ivory complexion and auburn coloring, which seemed to create more and more spots with each passing year.

Joshua's gaze traveled to the freckles on her nose and cheeks. "Those spots have captivated me for over a decade. Looking at your face is like gazing up at the stars. One could get lost in the beauty of its divine decree."

She blushed. No one had ever said anything so beautiful to her in her life. A snowflake fell and melted against her cheek and Phoebe looked toward the sky. Another landed on the tip of her nose and despite everything she was feeling, she smiled.

"I bet I can catch more snowflakes on my tongue than you can," Joshua challenged as he pulled himself up into the seat next to her and threw a fur blanket across her lap.

"That's a silly game," she replied.

"How can you say something you've never played is silly?"

"Because just the thought of us driving down the road with our tongues sticking out sounds childish, or at the very least scandalous."

He flicked the reins. "Like something the cousin of the scandalous sisters would do?" He inquired. She eyed him as they left the castle behind and he tilted his head toward the sky. Then he opened his mouth and stuck his tongue out.

Joshua had his tongue stuck out as if there was absolutely nothing improper about such a display in front of his employer, let alone a lady.

She stared at him, amazement and something she couldn't identify washing over her. She had seen many men act without a care for propriety, especially when it came to their behavior around scandalous women, but Joshua had never done anything so unaffected or frivolous in their entire acquaintance. The innocence of the act contradicted his raw masculinity and it was…

Mesmerizing.

He looked over at her and grinned, his tongue still sticking out in the cold air without a single flake caught. "Will you not join me in my endeavor?"

A snort escaped her lips and she covered her mouth, giggling through her glove at his awkward pronunciations. "You're talking with your tongue sticking out." Incongruity made her comment sound like a question.

A snowflake landed on his tongue and he celebrated with a whoop, his joy completely infectious. "You try it."

"I couldn't."

"You could." He stuck his tongue out once more and she couldn't resist. She tilted her head back and opened her mouth. Almost instantly a flake landed on her eyelash and her lip at the same time. She blinked several times as she licked her lip. "I did it," she announced her voice full of a childlike wonder she didn't recognize.

Joshua scoffed. "Not only did you cheat, but you also didn't really catch one."

"I did too, right on my upper lip."

His gaze dropped to her mouth and she couldn't stop her tongue from tracing across her skin where the snowflake had fallen.

"You'll never catch a snowflake like that," he rasped, his voice holding a huskiness she'd only heard once before, and she knew, without a doubt, she wanted so much more than a kiss on this sleigh ride.

"You must stick out your tongue and catch it." Still his gaze did not leave her mouth, as if the enticement to corrupt her into acting so wantonly was the most deliciously wicked thing he'd ever done.

And she was drawn by the potency of that desire. It was there in the dark depths of his gaze, the tautness of his jaw, while his lack of concentration on the horse displayed a natural ability to guide the sleigh as if it were no chore at all. He was masterful. Commanding. She did not want to disappoint this man who waited with bated breath as if her sticking out her tongue was the most erotic display he could ever wish to see.

Slowly, deliberately, she moistened her lips, tracing them one at a time. His nostrils flared as her teeth sunk into her lower lip and she slowly released it before leisurely sticking out her tongue bit by bit. Despite wanting to witness the intensity of his passion, she closed her eyes and savored the moment as she tilted her head back in pure abandon.

She'd only surrendered to temptation once in her lifetime. In her library. With him. Joshua made her want to carry on as if the world was hers, and not the other way around. This unrestrained freedom did not belong to women of the ton, and despite all her shocking and outrageous house parties, Phoebe had never once participated in such an unspeakable display of impropriety.

He did this to her. For her.

She let the silence of the snowfall engulf her. The sleek

runners of the sleigh, slicing through the deep snow. The clop of the horse's hooves mingled with the animal's heavy breath as it created a symphonic beat with the jingle of the sleigh bells that announced the coming of a new age for her. An age where she let down her guard and enjoyed the small gifts of life she'd never been allowed to acknowledge.

A small frozen dewdrop splashed on the warmth of her tongue, and then another, larger than the first. A smile spread across her face, and strong gentle fingers caressed her jaw, gliding upward into her hair as she was pulled toward Joshua. Her hand immediately grasped for something to hold onto, anything to give her stability in this unsettling new reality of truly wanting to give herself to another.

Her palm found the only thing that could possibly give her the security she needed—a powerful, muscular thigh. Lips crushed hers and she gasped, her eyes popping open to see Joshua up close and personal. The strength of his fingers flexing through her hair was intoxicating. Like a drug too potent to resist, his tongue took advantage of her shock and delved into her mouth, caressing her own with a carnality she had dreamt about for months.

To say she relaxed into his embrace would be a lie. She melted into it with as much pent-up passion as he. They combusted as one, their bodies aflame with desire, her eyes falling closed once more as her bonnet dropped from her head. His kiss grew bolder, deeper and she reveled in the heat of their passion. He was everything she had ever dreamed a lover could be. Giving. Wild and unrestrained. In any other lover, it would have been unsettling. With Joshua it made her bold.

She began kneading his thigh, gloried in the flexing of his long, unyielding muscles as she followed the path where she'd known this ride would lead, straight to his cock. Joshua groaned into their kiss as she traced the long, hard length of him. Strong and powerful, it strained under her touch, growing harder with each loving stroke of her hand and tempting her with everything she had coveted for years.

She pulled away from his kiss, startling him. Scaring him. His gaze searched hers for something like reproach for his bold impassioned kiss, and then he looked to where the horse had taken them. He still held the reins in one hand, but neither of them had been cognizant of their path.

The two of them were breathing hard, the distance between them nearly unbearable. Joshua immediately filled the silence as he stared forward. "I apologize. I should not have taken advantage of your person when you were vulnerable. I should have never lost control and taken such little care with your well-being."

She laughed. "If you will notice, Mr. Forrester, there are no cliffs in this particular region. The topography is treeless and rather flat."

"On the contrary, the scenery is full of tempting hills and valleys." His eyes roamed her form, hidden from his view by her redingote. But Joshua's muscular build was displayed magnificently with his great coat open, exposing his trousers to the elements and her view.

He truly was a masterpiece of masculinity.

"I won't apologize for what I'm about to do, despite the vulnerable position you are in," she said.

His eyes grew wide as she slipped to her knees in front of him. She watched as he surveyed the area for anyone who might be looking, but she knew there was no one there. She'd lived here for nearly nine months. Not a soul traveled to and from the castle from this direction. They were in the wilds of Scotland, where most Londoners would never be caught, and where the Scottish people had carved out their own little piece of paradise centuries ago.

This afternoon, on Nithesdale land, they would experience their own winter paradise. Carriages could not travel where they went, and sleighs were held only by the grand estates. The closest one to Caerlaverock was owned by the Earl of Astley, who had been traveling abroad for several months. No one would travel to Caerlaverock. Except Joshua, and he had come for her.

"Phoebe, what are you doing?"

"Fulfilling my list."

"This seems like it should be my list."

She raised her wrist to her mouth and slowly worked one button, then two at the top of her glove as she loosened them with her teeth. The intensity of his expression was everything she'd ever wanted. When the buttons were free of their mooring, she pulled one finger off at a time, nipping the tips of her glove with her teeth as she went. She tossed the glove onto the seat next to him and began to repeat the process with her second glove, but added a bit of temptation as she swirled her tongue around the buttons, enjoying where his thoughts strayed as she teased him with what she was about to do.

"You are captivating on an average day, but today, you could provoke a saint into being wicked."

"Am I corrupting a saint?"

"Hardly, but I will admit that I have never been so thoroughly enticed."

She tossed the second glove to the seat and he gazed into her eyes, not looking at her hands as she glided them up his thighs to the top button of his falls. She bypassed where they both wanted her to touch and made her way to his waistband, enjoying the muscle and sinew along the way. With each fastener she loosened, his cock grew harder, thicker, longer. It was magnificent and she had yet to see it in all its glory. Each button was a revelation in his desire and hers. She wanted to bring this man pleasure like no other.

The rise and fall of his chest grew faster, in tandem with the clop of the horse's hooves in the snow, and when she had finished unbuttoning his trousers, he couldn't resist any longer. He stared at her hands in avid fascination. It was all the permission she needed to watch the unveiling of his manhood as it strained against his drawers, and when it sprung loose from its cotton sheath, she nearly gasped at its allure. Never before had a man's cock held such appeal. He was indescribably beautiful in his masculinity, and an ache began to build in her core as she wrapped her hand around his girth.

Silken steel glided through her grip as her hand traveled the length of him from base to tip. When he let out a long, hard breath, her control vanished. She leaned in and took him in her mouth, savoring the taste and feel of him on her tongue as he groaned in pleasure.

"Holy fuck," he gasped.

"Not yet, this is just a prelude of what is to come," she told him and went back to fulfilling item number two on her list as she licked and nibbled and sucked every inch of his exposed flesh, including two very tight balls that did not qualify for snow at all.

Four

My New Year's Resolution List

1. Build a snowman of Mr. Forrester and make it anatomically correct of him in all his male glory.

2. Have a snowball fight with Mr. Forrester and take his snowballs in my hand and lick and taste a gentleman's jewels for the first time in my life.

3. Make a snow angel and let Mr. Forrester show me the way to the pearly gates with his tongue.

4. Ride a sled down a hill with Mr. Forrester riding me.

5. Go on a sleigh ride with Mr. Forrester racing at the reins and return the favor as I ride him.

6. Go on a long carriage ride with Mr. Forrester, and do every scandalous act I read about in those naughty books while he and I are traveling across the countryside.

—A most wanton New Year's resolution list written by Lady Phoebe Drake, meant for the eyes of the Duchess of Nithesdale, but read by Mr. Joshua Forrester instead. The list was not burned as intended. It was carefully placed inside the reader's pocket to be treasured for eternity.

Phoebe's mouth was on his cock.

Forget hell. He was definitely in heaven. He would have thought his cock would shrivel in the cold. To the contrary, her hands and mouth were heating him to a boiling point.

"You've never done this before?"

She gave a slight shake of her head and he felt her smile on his cock. Holy hell, that glorious smile. And it belonged to him.

"I find that impossible to believe," he croaked as her fingers heated his bollocks, causing them to tighten beyond comprehension. Her brow furrowed and he quickly clarified his statement. "What I mean to say..." He groaned once more as her tongue swirled around the length and the focused on the tip. "Phoebe," he gasped. "You are on the verge of unmanning me."

"That is the point, Joshua. Are you watching the road?"

"There is no bloody road," he rasped as he glanced around the field and attempted to see if there were any travelers about or hunters bringing a rabbit home to cook. His gaze was met with a winter wonderland more beautiful than he'd ever imagined, especially when his gaze returned to the fallen angel kneeling at his feet with her snow-covered auburn curls bent over his cock. Life was glorious and he was going to spend all over her if he wasn't careful.

"Phoebe." He sounded out of control and that wicked little grin of hers teased his cock once more before she began taking him deeper, harder, faster. His cock struck the back of her throat and she struggled for a moment but then flattened her tongue and continued as if she had been a trained courtesan. She was determined and glorious.

His spine tingled. His bollocks tightened. "Phoebe, I...I can't hold back."

She ignored his warning.

"I'm going to come." And he did. In her sweet, delectable mouth, he came like he never had before. His cock pulsing and spending like an untried lad with his first sexual experience. It was maddening to have so little control. He had thought to give her pleasure first. He had dreamed about making her come so many times, and she had been the one to be bold.

She leaned back on her heels and wiped the corners of her mouth with a single delicate finger as her tongue brushed across her upper lip and snow sprinkled down on her auburn curls. Then she slowly tucked his semi-hard cock back inside his trousers, each touch making him want more as she buttoned his falls. It had been impossible to take his eyes from her until she glanced forward and his own eyes followed her gaze.

"We are lucky this landscape is endless," he confessed. "I'm not sure I would have noticed a cliff."

A satisfied grin graced her lips as he helped her back into the seat, but she wouldn't be there long. Items number one and three on her list were about to become a reality. He spied the crumbled stone ruins of an ancient wall to his right and directed the horse to them before pulling on the reins to stop the sleigh.

"What are we doing?"

"You wanted to make a snowman, and I promised to help you fulfill your list."

"Iseabail said we should make a snow woman," Phoebe replied while putting on her gloves.

"It is your list. We will make whichever you desire."

"Then I would like to make both as they embrace in a kiss."

He lifted a brow. "I believe one part of the snowman you wanted to build won't be visible if they are kissing."

"Yes, but I will know where it will be buried."

"I like this saucy side of you," he said as he pulled the horse to a stop and hopped down from the sleigh.

He reached up and placed his hands on her waist to help her down and couldn't resist running her body down the length of his on her way to the ground. He groaned as her core came into contact with his quickly hardening cock and her eyes widened.

"So soon?"

"It is always hard with you around," he answered truthfully.

She scoffed. "I would have noticed."

"I can assure you, it's true."

She ran her hand over the length of him as if she could not believe he was ready once more. It was enough for him to decide the snow-couple could bugger off until another day. He had a snow angel to please. Joshua bent over and pick her up.

Phoebe squeaked. "What are you doing?"

"It's time for a snow angel."

"Here?"

"Here."

"But what if someone comes?"

"No one is coming, except you."

She giggled. "Joshua. I had no inkling you were so devilish."

"Let me show you how sinful I can be," he growled.

He traipsed through the ankle-deep snow and then carefully laid her down in the cold, soft layers of white. "Keep your feet together and your hands at your sides until I step toward your feet, then bring your arms out and over your head as you bring your legs as wide as your skirts will allow so that you erase my footprints. Then close your eyes and enjoy."

"What if I want to watch?"

"Then you may watch, but if you're able to keep your eyes open the entire time, I am doing something seriously wrong."

"Why is that?"

"Have you never experienced an orgasm?"

"I think so."

His brow knitted. "I will make certain you know so."

Phoebe closed her eyes as she moved her arms and legs back and forth. Her lashes twitched with each snowflake that landed on her peaceful expression. Watching her as snow sprinkled down on her form, adorning her hair, cheeks, and lashes as her grin grew with each passing stroke of her arms and legs was a lesson in erotic temptation. Her coat opened farther with each pass of her legs. Her gown was creeping upward exposing lengths of her wool stockings and the shapely form of her calves. A rumble of desire formed in his chest.

"This feels remarkable," she whispered. "Rousing and exhilarating."

She really didn't know how arousing it was. His cock was as hard as it had ever been. He wanted her here and now. In the wet snow with her arms and legs flung wide. Resisting was the biggest feat of self-control he'd ever experienced. What he wanted more was to taste her, destroy her walls and make her scream to the heavens in ecstasy.

Joshua dropped to his knees, pulled off his gloves and pushed her skirts to her waist. He held her legs apart as he exposed her lace-trimmed drawers and groaned. Only Phoebe would have the drawers of a courtesan and never allow anyone to see them but her maid. He would rather have seen her entire body bare to him, but he would settle for her sweet, bare cunny. He ran his hands up her thighs, to her waist and beyond, where her lush breasts strained against her redingote buttons. He could not wait to take them in his mouth, but for now he would satisfy himself with making her come. He rubbed her breasts through her clothing and she arched her back as he brought his face down to the opening in her drawers. He breathed in the sweet scent of her desire and closed his eyes as lust flowed through his body.

He massaged her breast with one hand as he pushed apart the slit in her drawers with the other, exposing her intimate wet lips. "Fuck me."

Phoebe froze and then lifted to her elbows and her eyes met his.

"Bend your knees," he instructed as he released her breast and brought both of his hands to her ankles and spread them wide, exposing even more of her flesh to him.

"You're ruining my angel," she breathed, her chest rising and falling in a brisk manner.

"An angel who looks like you *should* fall." His mouth hovered over her flesh as he savored her scent and allowed his warm breath to tease her with what he was about to do.

"Joshua." The plea fell from her lips and he answered it with a stroke of his tongue up her center. She bucked and gasped, and he put one hand on her lower abdomen, her reaction stoking a need in him he did not recognize. It was all consuming, never-ending, and he knew in that moment he would never get enough of Phoebe.

He would not let her escape their destiny now. Not after he had tasted how good life could be. He licked and licked, glorified in her pleasure as her legs began to quiver. He devoured her wetness like a man who had found the Garden of Eden in the middle of the icy-cold fields of Scotland. When he stuck his tongue inside her warm wet channel, a moan was torn from his lips with the pure decadence of the woman he loved.

Her back arched, her stomach tightened beneath his hand and her speech turned into incongruent murmurs of longing. "Ohhh," she sighed. "Ahhh." It was as if she could think of nothing else to say, and that was exactly where he wanted her. Her hand went to his head as she pushed his mouth against her core and it was his turn to smile on her most intimate parts.

He moved back to her clit, teasing and swirling his tongue in a manner to drive her to the edge. He was rewarded with a gasped, "Yes, oh God, yes."

Then he slid a finger inside her and her muscles contracted around it, sucking him inside as she let out a cry. He lapped at the soft, delicate skin of her sex, her taste making him harder than he thought possible. Phoebe shuttered. Her control slipping as her body trembled, and she fucked his face, calling out his name. "Joshua, please."

He flicked her clit without mercy, savagely driving his finger into her harder and harder, pushing her orgasm through the restraint of years of denial. "Come for me," he demanded, because he needed to feel her orgasm on his tongue like nothing he'd ever desired before in his life. "Come for me, Phoebe." He sucked on her clit and just as she began to shatter, he applied his teeth with just enough pressure to drive her over the edge.

"Joshua!" she screamed, his name a prayer on her lips as her hot core milked his fingers with her orgasm.

A harsh breath exploded from her lips and a laugh filled

the skies as he slowly brought her back down to earth, languidly stroking the receding quakes of her core.

"I have never felt *that* before."

Satisfaction flowed through his body, but he wasn't done with her. She needed to be ready for the next item on her list. He pushed her legs up higher and placed her feet on his shoulders. Her hand returning to his head.

"I don't think I could possibly..."

He shoved a second finger inside her and curled them, pushing on a place that drove her wild. She bucked and pumped against his face, his teeth scraping her clit, and her core tightened once more as her body began to quiver. Just when she was about to come, he removed his fingers and pulled his mouth away.

"No...no, no, no. Don't stop."

He ignored her plea, grabbed his gloves and stood up, taking her with him. Phoebe's cheeks were flushed pink, her eyes dilated and as dark as the distant forest. He smoothed down her skirts, turned her around and brushed the snow off her backside, nearly groaning as he was unable to resist plumping her tempting derriere with his palm. "Do you know what you do to me?" he asked as he pulled her toward the sleigh.

"What?" she asked.

"You make me want to go for a sleigh ride." He lifted her up into the sleigh, then grabbed the reins as he jumped into the red padded seat next to her.

With the flick of his wrists, they were gliding across the snow once more, their pace faster and more exhilarating.

Then Phoebe lifted her skirts to her waist, swung her leg over his thighs and she was straddling him. Rubbing her quim back and forth against the placard of his falls and he thrust his hips toward her in a powerless surrender to desire. Their eyes met, anticipation racing through his veins, their passion palpable between them. Her need for him as great as his was for her.

"After we are married, I will purchase us a sleigh," he whispered as he nuzzled her neck, her auburn hair draping them in a curtain of silken curls blowing in the wind.

She froze on top of him and pulled away from his kisses. "Married?"

She began to slide off his lap but he stilled her with one firm grip on her right thigh. "Damnation," he cursed. "I had this all planned out, but then you went down on your knees and—"

"This is my fault?" she asked.

"No! No, that's not what I'm saying at all. This is my fault for losing control." Years ago he had recognized Phoebe was his weakness. She would always have more control over his body than he did. If she wished, he would jump and it wasn't because she was his employer. He'd refused numerous seduction attempts by client's wives and lonely widows.

He slowed the horse to a trot and took a deep breath before continuing. "You are different than any other woman I've known. From the moment I met you so many years ago you have owned my heart and body."

Her eyes widened in disbelief. "You haven't been with another woman since we met?"

He shook his head. "I'm muddling this up. Yes, I've been with other women, but only because there was no hope for us. You were my employer and then you were with Nithesdale."

"I was never with Nithesdale."

"I know that now, but the way you two carried on, I thought... It doesn't matter what I thought. I know it wasn't true and I know why you pretended."

"You do?"

"Yes. Nithesdale told me a few years ago. He said you were protecting him. Restoring his reputation as a man while helping with Iseabail."

"I owed him."

"We all owed him so very much," he said quietly. The loss of the man they'd loved still stinging.

"Was he your father?"

It was his turn to be taken aback. "What would make you think that?"

"There are rumors he sired two bastards. I thought one of them might be you."

"No," he said, sadness tinging his voice. "He was the only father figure I've ever known, but Nithesdale only sired one bastard, and it was not me."

"Who?" she asked, curiosity obviously getting the best of her.

"It's not my story to tell. Only the child's mother can answer that question." When she started to speak, he put one finger on her lips and she sucked it into her mouth. It was one of the same fingers he had used to caress her inner walls and his cock twitched beneath her with the knowledge. Phoebe then began rubbing the soft round globes of her arse over the top of him and he nearly threw her from his lap to keep their conversation on track. Instead, he stilled her with one hand while still holding the reins in the other.

"Who's being the demon now?" he asked.

"You bring out the worst in me."

"I would say I bring out the best in you." He thrust up into her and she bent over to kiss him. He steeled himself against her charms and pulled away. "I want you more than I can possibly articulate, however, I will not fulfill number four or five on your list without a betrothal in place."

Her brow furrowed. "I thought we had agreed marriage was not necessary."

"We never agreed. I said I understood your reservations. You were left in a horrible predicament after Richard died. Women are treated abominably by society and the world over, but that does not mean I will use you in the basest of manners and be done. I told you that I love you, and I meant it. Those were not mere words. While you were upstairs at Caerlaverock, I wrote up a marriage contract."

Nothing could have frightened her more than him uttering the word *marriage*. He knew that and she began to fight to lift her right leg to the other side of the seat once more. He used his strength against her for the first time, holding her in place on his lap.

"I cannot—"

"It is within your purview to cut me out of your life, but I beg of you to read the contract. I know you care for me. I've seen it in your eyes, felt it in your caress, and absorbed it on my tongue. You are not a woman who has casual relations. I know this. You care. You may not love me, but you care deeply for me. More than you ever did for Richard, or Nithesdale."

At her sharp intake of breath, he continued. "I love you. Take the contract from my pocket and read how much I love you and respect you. If you do not want to marry me after reading it, I will take you back to the castle and never mention it again."

She searched his eyes, looking for the trap she was afraid he would spring, but he did not back down, nor did he show any weakness, just the love he'd felt for so many years.

She reached inside his pocket, and with his heart pounding, fear and arousal coursing through his body with equal measure, she pulled out the contract. He briefly closed his eyes and said a prayer. This was it. Everything he'd ever wanted would be decided in the next few moments and part of him wished he had ten more years to convince her to be his.

Five

Marriage Contract

On this seventh day of December in the year of our Lord 1811, Mr. Joshua Forrester, Esquire, of London, England, of sound mind and character pledges to Lady Phoebe Drake of Mayfair, England, as a testament of his commitment to maintaining a strong and enduring marriage, the following provisions:

1. Lady Drake will maintain sole proprietorship of Lady Atwood's Millinery shops along with all its properties and financial holdings.

2. Lady Drake will continue to be the sole proprietor of Drake Manor and all its holdings to include furniture, livestock, and lands.

3. If the marriage results in children Lady Drake will be

the sole decision maker in how the familial coffers are distributed to the children.

4. Mr. Forrester will sign over half of his properties and financial holdings, along with half of the Dickenson Mayer & Forrester legal firm to Lady Drake upon marriage.

This marriage contract serves as a testament to our commitment to maintaining an enduring and supportive marriage. By entering into this agreement, the parties involved pledge to uphold the values of trust, loyalty and mutual respect.

Signed Mr. Joshua Forrester seventh day of December 1811

Signed

—a marriage contract between Mr. Joshua Forrester and Lady Phoebe Drake written in haste but with the deepest respect for the woman he loved by Mr. Joshua Forrester, Esquire.

She was straddling him in a most indecent manner as only a wanton widow would do, yet she couldn't regret it. Ever. She read the contract a second time through, looking for a loophole only a solicitor would see. Joshua had taught her what to look for, but what if in this instance he hid something in plain sight?

She grabbed hold of the obvious. "I can't have children."

"They aren't a necessity."

"You don't want a son?"

"I would love a son or a daughter, but whether we have children or not has no bearing on my desire to marry you. What if I am incapable of producing a child? Would that have any bearing on your desire to marry me?"

"Of course not, but most men don't want to marry a widow whose marriage produced no offspring."

"Most men don't love you the way I do. I want to share my life with you. Work together, play together, wake up with you in my arms every day and grow old with you. If we are graced with children they will only add to our happiness. If we are not, my joy of spending my life with you will not be diminished."

"Most men want my land, my house, my belongings, my business. My money."

"Then they are blind and ignorant. I want you. Only you. Why else would I give you half of everything I possess?"

She didn't know. Even her parents hadn't loved her enough to give her funds of her own. They had given it all to Richard. True, the marriage contract had said everything reverted to her upon his death, but he had run everything into the ground by then.

A tear ran down her cheek and Joshua wiped it away with the brush of his thumb. More tears followed and he gently brushed them away as well.

"No one has ever thought of my needs before their own," she said in a voice that wavered with every syllable.

"I will always put your needs before my own."

She stared into his fathomless eyes that seemed more stalwart than she had ever seen before. "And who will put your needs first?" She would of course, but she needed to know what he expected.

"I am content at being second, or third, or fourth."

"Why would you be third or—oh." The hope that was blossoming in her chest died. "I cannot have children, Joshua."

"Then I will be second. It matters not."

Her chin began to quiver and he placed a gentle, consoling kiss on her lips which only made her tears fall faster.

He pulled back and gazed into her eyes once more, his expression serious and, to be honest, frightening. "I need you to understand that you won't be able to travel in the same social circle you are accustomed to if you marry me."

She laughed at his fear. She shouldn't, yet it was so preposterous, she couldn't stop that single bit of hope from escaping as she rushed to reassure him. "You do realize the scandalous set I belong to, don't you? They will continue to accept me, provided I continue to throw the house parties *they* are accustomed to."

A wrinkle appeared on his brow and she was certain he would change his mind. "Can I request that we reduce the number of parties to two parties a year?"

"As my husband, you may insist we throw zero parties a year." She prayed he wouldn't try to be so controlling. That was not a relationship she cared to have.

"I would not do that to you."

"I wouldn't mind if you did." Because in this instance, if she was being honest, she didn't.

His forehead smoothed as if he finally understood what she was saying. "Does that mean you will marry me?"

Joy blossomed in her chest in a manner she'd never experienced. It felt as if she would explode with the pure wonder of the moment, and she smiled. "Yes, I will marry you, Joshua."

He kissed her then. It wasn't gentle, or soothing. Their lips crashed together hard, with her claiming him with an equal amount of vigor. He suddenly drew back.

"You have to sign it."

"What?"

"You have to sign the contract."

She laughed, her bubble of joy bursting from the seam of her lips. "What exactly do you plan to use for quill and ink?"

His eyes twinkled. "My inkstand is in the travel compartment to my right."

"You thought of everything."

"I aim to please." He ground against her and her breath caught. Every part of her that wanted a repeat performance of that *petite mort* she'd been gifted just moments ago, tingled with anticipation of joining with him for the first time.

She pulled the fur off the seat next to them and removed the cushion. Hidden from view was a compartment large enough to hold a pistol. Joshua's weapon of choice sat inside, his gorgeous gilt bronze inkstand with a handle in the form of a serpent.

"Nithesdale always said you wielded a deadly pen."

"I hope this one is filled with life, love and promise." He pulled her tight against his cock with his free hand.

She removed his quill and the inkstand while trapping the marriage contract between their bodies. "You are not making this easy." Her lip quirked.

"I want you to know your mind and know that you are certain about your decision."

"I have trusted you for nearly a decade, it was myself whom I did not trust."

"And now?"

"I don't believe I could make a better decision for my future."

He let out a long, sweet breath as if he had been holding it for years. He kissed her then and she nearly spilled the ink over the two of them before he pulled away. "Sorry," he said but the look in his eyes was anything but apologetic. He looked as if he would ravish her if she didn't sign the contract quickly. "You're torturing me, Phoebe love."

Phoebe love. Had any two words sounded more beautiful? More decadent? She rubbed against him, torturing them both and she closed her eyes with the wonderful sensation.

"Phoebe." Her name was a petition on his lips.

She set the inkstand down on the seat and dipped the quill in the inkpot. Then she held the marriage contract on the wide expanse of his chest and signed her name. It was neither neat nor elegant, but it was hers.

She looked up into his face and found his gaze riveted on

her signature. "We don't have a witness," she whispered, too afraid the moment might shatter if she spoke too loudly.

"Gentlemen don't require a witness when negotiating a marriage contract for a bride. I hardly see where a bride and groom would require one if both are of sound mind and body, and neither have a guardian."

That was just one of the reasons why she loved him; they were equal in their decision-making, fifty-fifty. It was why she had loved him and trusted him like no other for years, yet she'd been too afraid to acknowledge it. But no more. "I love you, Joshua Forrester. You are a man who recognizes a woman's capabilities and helps her reach her potential without judgement of her because of her sex."

"Can you say that again?"

"You are a man—"

"No. Not that part."

She grinned wickedly, teasing him with false naiveté. "What part?"

He pinched her backside. "You minx, the other part."

"I love you, Joshua Forrester."

"Put the powdered gum sandarac on the contract and let's get down to business."

"Business?" she asked with a cant of her hips.

"Completing New Year's resolutions can be arduous work," he replied.

"I hope you plan to work exceedingly *hard* at it," she said as she sprinkled the sand on her signature and blew on the ink. "I think the sand froze on the vellum."

"Leave it. Put it all back in the compartment before I lose control and paint us with ink."

"Of course, husband." Her lips quirked as she carefully placed the container of sand into the inkstand and then returned everything to the compartment with the addition of their marriage contract. She threw the latch and Joshua snapped the reins several times. His Royal Highness responded, galloping across the field at an exhilarating speed.

"You do realize that you will have to do most of the work at this speed?"

"That's exactly how I fantasized about it."

A growl was torn from his lips as she reached down and undid the falls of his trousers. She sat on his lap facing him, his arms encompassing her in an embrace as he drove the sleigh across the field. "You are a woman with all the power to wreck me."

"Keep your eyes on the pasture so that is the only way we wreck."

His brow dipped in concentration. "I will not risk your safety."

"That's why I would only do this with you at the reins." She freed the length of him from his garments and ran her hand up and down his shaft. She couldn't help but admire his strength and power and wondered if this position would be too much with a man like Joshua.

She looked up at his face and saw the tightening of his jaw. "Are you well?"

"I am beyond well, but I would love to be inside you fulfilling your wish."

"Is it only my wish?" she asked as she began stroking him faster, her hand increasing the pressure.

"Bloody hell, woman. Stop that and get on top."

"Byron would be jealous of your prose," she smirked.

"Byron would be jealous of my position. He could only dream of having such an enticing goddess on his lap."

"You don't need to flatter me."

He met her gaze, his wild, unruly passion kept at bay behind a mask of seriousness. "It's not flattery when a man speaks the truth. Don't ever doubt my words when I speak of you." His handsome visage never looked so stunning as it did in that moment and she had never desired anything more than to make him hers.

She lifted to her knees and opened the slit of her drawers to allow his body entry as she positioned him at her core. Rubbing the tip of his cock against her, she drew pleasure from his warmth, his enticing sleek cock stood as hard as before. From the exquisite feel of his thick manhood against her feminine folds, the desire she'd felt mere minutes ago in the freezing snow returned. She grew slick and wet, his tip sinking into her with a tightness that thrilled her.

Lord, she wanted to take him inside her and never let him leave. She hadn't even brushed the brink of bliss, and yet she was consumed by the feel of him. It was as if they were soaring through the sky. Reaching for the heavens as one as she sunk down upon his heat, trembling with the intensity and fullness of taking in all of him. He breathed out a heavy breath in a whoosh. The sensations overwhelming them both, she bit down on his neck as her hair tumbled around them. Pleasure surged through her body as brisk winter air swirled around them.

Joshua reached up with one hand and tore her redingote and gown open from the neck down to her waist. Phoebe gasped, the act a complete shock from the man who had shown so much control over the years of their relationship. Her reaction did not stop him. He was a man on a mission of passion as he freed her from her corset and chemise, baring her to the elements. The cold was bracing, invigorating as he peered down to admire her full breasts.

She lifted and sank down on him, filling herself beyond what was comfortable, yet it was so desirable, she couldn't stop. She began riding him as if her life depended on it. Her breasts bouncing in the cold winter air. He lifted one, her breast spilling over his palm as he brought it to his mouth to suck and tease, taunting her with tantalizing swirls of his tongue.

She groaned with the pleasure of it. She felt completely vulnerable yet protected just the same. The emotions were staggering. Consuming. Never before had she felt so much control and so little at the same time. He released her breast and reached down between them, lust overtaking her as he found the pleasurable nub at her apex. She flexed her hips and grabbed the rear of the sleigh for balance. Her knees shook as he held the reins with one hand like it was something he did all the time.

"You are more beautiful right now than I've ever seen you," he said on a rasp and the beginning of her orgasm washed away her remaining restraint. Her body humming, she swiveled her hips and he moaned with satisfaction. She was panting with each rise and fall on his cock, riding him across the countryside at a pace she'd never imagined she could. Her breasts bounced and flounced, and she loved it. The intensity of his hunger as he tried to keep his eyes on where they were going—but couldn't as his gaze strayed to her nakedness—sent her over the edge. The raw carnality causing her back to arch as her body quaked, her sheath convulsing around him.

Joshua grunted, his jaw tightening, the tendons on his neck visible as he let out a fierce roar. His free hand wrapped around her, under her arm and up across her back to grasp the top of her shoulder, holding her in place as he thrust upward with so much aggression, on anyone else it would be frightening. On him it was intoxicating. His furious thrusts shifted their position and sent her body singing with plea-sure. The spasms of bliss she never dreamed were possible, pulsing through her core once more as he drove into her, rocking his body against her clit, and she screamed a second release. Her voice mixing with his in the countryside, an erotic chorus of wantonness and satisfaction.

Phoebe fell against his chest, his chin resting on her head, both breathing hard as if they were the ones to pull the sleigh through the deep snow, and not the horse. Joshua slowed the horse to a trot, wrapping his arm around her and pulling her tight.

"I'm sorry. I should have never lost control like that," his apology said on a ragged breath. "I didn't mean to expose you."

She pulled back and looked him in the eyes. Concern, and was that fear clouding his expression?

"Don't you dare apologize for what we just did. I have never felt more alive than what I have in the past hour with you." She kissed him then, hard and demanding, letting him know he was exactly who she wanted. Needed. Desired.

When she pulled back, a satisfied grin crossed her lips and he searched her face for the lie. But there wasn't one. There would never be one. Not between them. Only truth.

His expression softened until he realized she was bare to the elements and he stopped the horse with a deep, "Whoa."

Then he was pulling up her chemise and corset, and attempting to close the front of her torn gown and redingote with little success. "If you become sick, I will never forgive myself."

"If I become sick it won't be from the fresh air of the Scottish countryside."

He stood up, giving her little choice but to wrap her legs around his middle, his cock still buried inside her, as he put one hand under her backside. "Damn, but you challenge a man's stamina."

She clamped her inner walls around him and he groaned. "Minx."

"Devil," she replied when his cock flexed inside her.

"This must wait, until I get you back to the warmth of Caerlaverock." He lifted her off his quickly hardening shaft and placed her in the middle of the fur. Then he pulled it over the top of her head and wrapped the ends around her, covering her from the tip of her nose to the tip of her toes.

"How will you stay warm?" she asked as he buttoned the falls of his trousers, stuffing his sex down into the fabric with difficulty.

"As hot as that exercise in debauchery made me, it will take me several hours to get my body temperature back to normal." He dropped a kiss on her lips before sitting in the seat next to her and flicking the reins.

"I cannot wait to fulfill my next resolution."

He grinned. "Neither can I."

Six

Dear Cousin,

It was good to hear that you are well, especially after encountering Napoleon's men on a mission of revenge. I am familiar with the Earl of Astley, and although I knew him to be intelligent, I believed his ruse of being a complete and utter wastrel and rogue. It's fascinating how wrong one can be, although I believe he will always qualify as a rogue.

I have never met the Countess of Astley, however, a client of mine is acquainted with her and I will request she accompany me to notify the countess of her son's predicament. My client is very kind-hearted and I have no doubt she will assist the countess through this difficult time. By the time you receive this missive, I will have met with the countess and hopefully the earl will have been returned to his family.

Journey safely, and may this war end quickly so that I may see you once again,

Joshua

—A letter to American Captain Miles Gallagher of the Fairhaven merchant ship from Joshua Forrester, Esquire, London, England, in reference to the capture of Simon Clark, Earl of Astley, December 1811

Prior to their return, Joshua had told Phoebe to stay in the sleigh until he lifted her out. The lad from the stable met them at the gate and took the reins to the horse.

"The price of exposing a lady to the Scottish winters," Joshua confessed to the two footmen standing guard.

"Yes, sir," one replied as he opened the gate. "The English do have difficulty adjusting to the brisk Scottish air."

"Nothing a hot bath won't cure," he said over his shoulder. Phoebe's shoulders shivered, but he knew it wasn't from the cold. She was desperately attempting to hold back a nervous laugh. If the footmen snickered or rose an eyebrow at his statement, he didn't notice and Phoebe certainly couldn't see from beneath the fur. Her face was buried too deeply into the lapel of his coat to see any of the guards.

He carried his bride-to-be over the threshold of Caerlaverock Castle not caring what the footmen at the gate thought about the spectacle he was creating. They entered the grand hall just as the Duchess of Nithesdale came out of the breakfast room.

The duchess's eyes grew wide. The pure horror of her expression sending a frisson of fear through his body. Then he realized how they would look to anyone who had not seen him lift Phoebe from the sleigh.

"Lady Phoebe is fine, Your Grace. Just a bit too much snow and cold for one day. I will take her upstairs to her room where the servants may prepare a hot bath and restore her to her spirited self." He pinched Phoebe's lush, round bottom beneath the furs where his hand wasn't visible and she squeaked in response.

He thought the duchess would have found humor in Phoebe's reaction, but she continued to gape at him with a look of chilly panic crossing her face. He stopped at the bottom of the steps.

"Is something wrong, Your Grace?"

Phoebe pushed her head from the furs and his gaze got caught on the enticing view of her mussed hair and rosy cheeks. She was sexy as hell in her current state, but she only had eyes for the duchess.

"Joshua, put me down," she instructed, her tone that of an employer and his heart nearly skidded to a stop. When he did not react, she repeated, "Joshua, put me down." The authority in her voice unmistakable and his heart sank with her decision. The duchess's shock at seeing them together must have made her realize her mistake. He'd known he was not of her station, but he had truly believed she didn't care. He'd apparently been wrong.

He immediately put her down on the first step. "My apologies, Lady Drake."

She glanced at him and the moment she saw the expression on his face, she rolled her eyes. "The duchess *needs* me."

"I don't know what to say. This is most embarrassing," the duchess interrupted.

Why was she embarrassed? He was the one to make a fool of himself. The one who had reached beyond his scope.

"I think we need to get you upstairs and get you comfortable so that you are prepared," Phoebe said.

The sound of water trickling onto the floor from beneath the duchess's gown changed everything. He suddenly understood her look of shock and horror, the red blotches of mortification appearing high on her cheeks. He was at her side in an instant, bending to put his arm under her legs. The duchess began to step away until a stab of pain rounded her shoulders forward over her protruding belly. She began breathing heavily, her chest rising and falling at a rapid pace, and a scream was torn from her lips. It was the most horrifying noise Joshua had ever heard in his life. Without further hesitation, he put one arm underneath her knees and the other behind her back. He lifted the duchess into his arms and headed for the stairs.

"Mrs. Hagerty!" Phoebe yelled as Joshua took the steps two at a time and reached the top of the steps faster than he thought possible, considering the awkward way in which the duchess had her arms wrapped around his neck in what felt like a stranglehold. He wasn't certain either one of them would survive much more of her delivery if he didn't get her to her bedchamber quickly. Due to the former duke's long illness, he was familiar with the layout of the family wing and he strode down the hall with the duchess panting in his arms, while Phoebe attempted to match his pace.

"Yes, Lady Drake?" the housekeeper said from the other end of the hallway.

"It's time," Phoebe said, her voice full of the same authority that had nearly scared him out of his wits moments ago.

"Time?" The housekeeper seemed confused until her gaze landed on him carrying the duchess. "Oh! Yes, my lady. I will call for the midwife immediately and make sure the maids bring in plenty of linens."

Joshua knew the basics of childbirth, but he was starting to learn more than he ever thought he would in his lifetime. Children had not been in his thoughts of the future at all. A wife had just recently become a possibility, let alone reality.

"This is most embarrassing. I do apologize for ruining your clothing, Mr. Forrester." The duchess attempted to straighten his cravat.

"I did that, not you," Phoebe stated. Her voice so matter-of-fact even the duchess took a moment to process the meaning.

"Oh. Ohhhhhh." She looked up at him.

"She has agreed to be my wife," he explained.

The duchess smiled. A wistful look of longing crossing her features and he suddenly felt like a heel for bringing it up at a time when she would be bringing her first child into the world alone.

"My apologies, Your Grace. I didn't mean to be insensitive."

"Don't apologize for being in love with my best friend, Forrester. I am very happy the two of you have finally acknowledged your feelings. It also explains the state of her hair and her gown."

"Once a scandal, always a scandal," Phoebe said as she opened the doors to the duchess's bedchamber.

The duchess and Phoebe could have been sisters. Both had long, coppery hair that captured a man's attention as soon as they walked into the room. With golden flecks glinting in the candlelight, it was as if their curls were burnished with fire. Before the duchess had become heavy with child, her tall, lithe form and quiet demeanor gave off an air of fragility despite her inner strength. Phoebe was the exact opposite, petite in nature, with voluptuous curves and a personality that embodied her sexuality.

Her lady's maid, Mary, scurried into the room after them, and Phoebe directed her as if she were the lady of the castle, a role he had seen her play countless times before. "The duchess has gone into labor. I believe we have prepared for this momentous occasion. Please start stripping the bedclothing."

The only other man in the castle, Paddington appeared at his side. "Can I be of assistance, Your Grace?" The elderly man was more of a grandfather figure to the duchess than a servant in her employ. The concern on his face was evidence of the love they shared.

The duchess, however, was unable to respond as she stiffened and began breathing heavily in his arms.

"The midwife should be here at any moment, Iseabail," Phoebe assured her.

"Please don't leave me, Phoebe." The duchess reached out for Phoebe's hand and Joshua had to stop for the women to hold hands. It would've been a touching moment, if he wasn't scared out of his wits that he would drop the awkwardly-shaped duchess. He needed to get her to the bed before another contraction came over her.

As if he thought the birth pang into existence, he felt the quivering of her stomach right before the duchess began yelling, "Oh my God, this child is going to kill me. Is this what it's always like? Do all women go through this amount of pain? I can't do this."

Joshua felt her stomach seizing and wondered how anyone could deal with the unrelenting violence traveling through their body. If he didn't put her down soon, he wasn't certain he could stomach what was to come next. "You will be fine, Duchess. You are a strong woman, you can do this," he said.

"How many...births have you attended, Mr. Forrester?" The duchess was now looking at him, and he wished he hadn't said a word because he wasn't certain his face didn't show the panic seeping in.

"I have known many women who have given birth to children."

A snort echoed through the bedchamber, and he glanced over at the source and found Phoebe openly smiling at him. It was the first time she had shown any emotion since they'd entered the castle. "Spoken like a true solicitor. I will take that response as meaning you have been present for exactly zero childbirths."

"My sister has given birth to three boys." His tone was defensive to his own ears.

"I never knew you had a sister. I just assumed you were an only child."

"Can we please focus on getting me into the bed? I have humiliated myself enough for one day," the duchess panted.

He began to lay her down on the bed, but she stopped him.

"Not in here. I should have Nithesdale's baby where he took his last breath."

Joshua looked down at the duchess and asked, "Are you certain?"

She took two quick breaths and nodded her head, too caught up in the contraction to respond verbally. Phoebe ran to the adjoining door and opened it to duke's bedchamber. The room looked exactly as it had the last time Joshua had been in the castle the month the duke had passed. The duchess had once compared the bedchamber to the *Gallerie des Glaces* at Versailles. Although she had never been to the French court, her mother had, and had described the Hall of Mirrors to her daughters in great detail.

The opulent chandelier in the ducal chamber glittered like a sky full of diamonds as it reflected light coming through the windows. The large golden bed had the Nithesdale crest embroidered on the deep blue canopy. Matching curtains hung over the floor-to-ceiling windows and were tied back with gold cords. Two gilded chairs sat in front of the fireplace where the duke and duchess used to sit and play chess before the fire. The board had been left with the pieces in position from the last game they had not completed prior to the duke's death. Joshua had always wondered if she would finish the game, but a silver box sat in the middle of the board, the black king guarding one side and the white queen on the other. Clearly, she had not. It was another piece of evidence to the duchess's dedication to her husband.

Paddington followed them into the room, the elderly butler breathing harder than the duchess. "Your Grace, if I may, the midwife is arriving as I speak. Mrs. Hagerty has started boiling water and the maids will be bringing in clean bed linens."

Phoebe pushed forward past Paddington and began pulling the expensive crested bed linens off the large bed with the assistance of Mary. Joshua then set the duchess down on the edge and she looked up at him with a look of appreciation and embarrassment. "If a duchess can be brought low, then I have certainly sunk into the depths today. I apologize, Forrester."

Joshua looked down at the soiled front of his best suit and couldn't help but smile. "I would wager that I am the first solicitor to ever participate in the birth of a peer, and I have the evidence to prove it."

"As I said, I ruined your suit. Any subsequent damage by the duchess is a conversation that will never leave this room," Phoebe said with a pointed look at him, Paddington and Mary, and they all nodded in agreement. "Now, if you could be so kind as to vacate the room so that I may undress Her Grace."

"I think you should probably let Mary help get me undressed while you attend your own gown," the duchess said with a hint of humor in her voice.

Phoebe looked down at her torn clothing which the fur was no longer concealing and inhaled sharply before snatching the wrap closed around her neck. Despite her bravado, Joshua knew she was rattled by her current state of dishabille.

"I will return shortly," she said as a bevy of women entered the room. Joshua wasn't certain who left the room quicker, him, Paddington or Phoebe, but as they left, a cacophony of noise erupted. Leading the pack was a woman in her fifties who was as round as she was tall. Her cap was slipping off a nest of graying hair, and her cheeks were rosy from exertion. Her eyes sparkled with good humor, and a booming voice rose above the other women.

"I believe it's time to bring in a new generation of the peerage. Are you ready, Duchess?"

Paddington closed the doors to the ducal bed chamber, and he and the butler slumped against a door as Phoebe ran down the hall to what he realized was her bedchamber. He and Paddington looked at one another.

"I need a brandy," Joshua admitted.

"The duke gave me a bottle to keep for this moment," Paddington confessed.

"Nithesdale gave you a bottle of brandy to open on the night his child was to be born?"

"Yes, sir. His Grace said that no duke could be born without drama surrounding his birth, and that I should imbibe for him at that moment."

"Nithesdale believed he was having a son?"

"As His Grace always said, 'You must have faith that everything will work out just as it was meant to be. The duchess will bear my heir.'"

Joshua shook his head in wonder. "Then I suggest we prepare ourselves for a long night with the brandy His Grace provided."

A scream interrupted Paddington's response, and he nodded his head once toward the stairwell. Joshua didn't need to be told twice. This was not a place for men, at least not the two men escaping to the lower rooms of the castle.

The sun crested the trees and a baby wailed with his first breath of life. "We have a new duke, Your Grace. Your husband would be very proud."

A sob tore from Iseabail's lips as she fell back onto the pillows and held her hands out for her son. Phoebe wiped away the sweat from her friend's forehead and then sat down next to her as the midwife brought the baby to Iseabail.

"He's absolutely gorgeous," Phoebe said as she swiped at the tears escaping down her cheeks.

Iseabail laughed as she cried, "He's the ugliest, most adorable child I've ever seen in my life."

"Have you thought about what you're going to name him?" asked Phoebe.

"Yes. I'm going to name him after his father and his grandfathers. Edward Xavier Blair Hancock."

Phoebe smiled and more tears fell down her cheeks. "Nithesdale would be so proud."

The midwife helped Iseabail place the baby at her breast, and the new Duke of Nithesdale nudged around before latching on and beginning to suckle.

"I didn't realize you planned to nurse your baby," Phoebe said.

"My mother breastfed every one of her daughters, except for Robina. It was a bond that she said could never be replaced. And once you get to know my youngest sister, you will understand how she seems a bit lost without the experience. Since Xavier will be my only child, I will not let him feel that loss."

"You don't know Xavier will be your only child."

Iseabail smiled down at her son, but there was a deep sadness that accompanied it. "Without his father, I cannot imagine having another. Now, if you could go down and tell Forrester the good news, I would be in your debt."

"Do you think he's still here? He was gone when I came back from changing."

Iseabail gazed down at her son, a sense of wonder and heartbreak visible in her expression. "Forrester was more nervous than all of us combined. He needs to know that he will represent the Duke of Nithesdale for decades to come."

"I don't think that was his first concern, do you?"

Iseabail shook her head, but couldn't take her eyes off her newborn son. "No, he is too good of a man for that, and that is why he will always represent this family."

Phoebe leaned over and kissed her friend's forehead before leaving the room and heading downstairs to the drawing room. She wasn't sure if Joshua was still at the castle, but if he was, she wanted to be the one to give him the good news. She pushed open the door to the drawing room and found the fire had burned down in the fireplace. The candle on the small writing desk was extinguished, and only the glow of the embers from the fire illuminated the room.

She looked toward the chair in the corner and found Joshua with his head back and his mouth slightly ajar. He was no longer wearing the soiled great coat and undercoat he had been wearing when he ascended the steps carrying Iseabail. His cravat was gone and his shirt sleeves were rolled up. He was the most tempting sight she had seen in her entire life. She walked over and whispered so that she did not startle him. "Joshua, are you awake?"

Unfocused eyes blinked up at her, and it took a moment for recognition to set in. His lips closed and he sat up, brushing a hand through his hair. He looked around the room and suddenly became aware of his surroundings. Then he stood up and wrapped her in his arms. "My apologies, darling. I did not mean to fall asleep. How is Her Grace?"

"Don't you mean, how is His Grace?"

Joshua frowned, his brows drawing together until the

meaning of her words sunk in and a brilliant but sleepy smile lit up his face. "It's a boy?"

"Edward Xavier Blair Hancock was born about thirty minutes ago."

"And Her Grace, she's doing well?"

"She is perfect."

"She told me it was a boy. I just didn't think things would work out so well for her. I mean, I had hoped that they would, but I've been surrounded by so much bad news of late, I guess I just didn't have faith in it."

It was Phoebe's turn to frown. "What bad news?"

He stepped away from her and ran a hand over his face. "The reason I came to Caerlaverock in the first place was to ask you to accompany me to Astley's estate in Hawick."

"Now? I can't go now. You know I can't leave Iseabail. She needs me. Why in the world would I possibly leave her during the holidays when she just gave birth?"

"Because I know the Countess of Astley was good to you during your first season and she's going to need you now more than ever."

The deep sense of calm she'd been feeling moments ago slipped into foreboding at the serious tone of his voice. It could only mean one thing. "Astley? Is he...?" She couldn't say the words because the Earl of Astley was the most irksome, obnoxious, joyous and fun-loving person she'd ever met. He'd also been responsible for saving the young life of Iseabail's sister when bandits ambushed her and her husband on their honeymoon. Caillen's husband had not survived the attack and it had taken Caillen months to recover.

Forrester shook his head. "He's not dead, at least not that I know of, but he's been kidnapped by the French and is being held for ransom by Napoleon himself."

Seven

Dear Joshua,

It is no secret that I have viewed you as a son. I could never openly love my own child without destroying his future, and when Dickenson Mayer presented you as my new solicitor, how could my broken heart resist you as a surrogate? My loneliness, however, came at a cost to your reputation. You have kept my secrets over the years, and for that I am eternally grateful.

Since the moment I introduced you to the young Lady Drake to assist her with her financial affairs, I was aware of your infatuation. I have watched your love for her grow over the years, but I believe if I did not know you as well as I do, I would have never noticed your hidden admiration and longing for something more. Your regard for her and her station are admirable qualities, and to any other member of the working class, I would not encourage a suit.

Yet I am also quite close with Lady Drake as well, I apologize for the masculine pride of an old man that has hindered your path. Allowing you, and many others, to believe she was more than a confidant was wrong of me. Lady Drake is, and will always be, a woman above reproach. Do not doubt what your heart is telling you. Lady Drake cares more deeply for you than she has any other living soul. Of that you can be certain.

It is up to you, dear boy, to win the lady. She has led a life of solitude for too long, and so have you. There has never been a couple more deserving of happiness than the two of you, and I pray you find the fortitude to break the boundaries of propriety and offer for the woman you love. As you know, I failed the woman I loved in life, and I hope to rectify that in death.

If you offer for the lady, I hope you will allow my duchess to give you a gift for the ceremony as a token of my love for the two of you and my blessings on your union.

With fatherly affection,
Nithesdale

—A letter to Mr. Joshua Forrester, Esquire, from Edward Charles Hancock, Duke of Nithesdale, written December 1810 a week before his death. A letter he gave to Joshua to open upon his death.

Phoebe walked into Iseabail's room and smiled at her friend who snuggled with her newborn baby. The midwife was gone and the young mother had returned to her own bedchamber. Iseabail was in a fresh dressing gown that was pulled down over one shoulder as she nursed her son, the new Duke of Nithesdale.

"Are you truly not going to use a wet nurse at all?"

"No, my parents may not have been the best at planning for their children's future, but I had a lovely childhood filled with laughter and love. I want my son to grow up experiencing those same warm family bonds, even if he won't have a father to race in the meadow or teach him to hunt and fish. I plan to do all those things with him as my father did with his girls."

"It doesn't need to be that way, Iseabail. You can have more children. You can remarry."

Iseabail's chin quivered as she caressed her son's black hair. "I will not risk his future or mine by putting doubt into the minds of the ton as to who should be the Duke of Nithesdale. Xavier is Edward's son, but his previous heir will attempt to prove he is not and I don't wish to give him any fuel to start any rumors."

Phoebe decided to drop the subject for now. Iseabail was feeling protective of her newborn son, and that was a good emotion for her to have. "Other than fishing and hunting and running through the fields, what other unladylike things do you plan on sharing with Xavier? Don't tell me you plan on cutting down your own Christmas tree?"

Iseabail smiled as she pulled Xavier from her breast and

began patting his back as if she had done it her entire life. "I will not be wielding an ax, but I will teach him to use a pen so that he may write his own resolutions."

"Speaking of resolutions..." Phoebe pressed her lips together to keep a giggle from startling the baby.

Her friend glanced up, a twinkle glistening in her eyes. "Your list was much naughtier than what Forrester read out loud to me, wasn't it?"

Phoebe couldn't help but tease her. "For being a widow who just gave birth, you have a one-track mind."

Iseabail adopted her most bewildered expression as she rapidly batted her eyelashes in a practiced look of innocence. "But you're the one who corrupted me, remember?"

"I believe we corrupted each other."

"True. But seriously, you must tell me what was on that list."

"We had this same discussion when you became pregnant. You said, and I quote, 'There are some things that should remain between a man and a woman. To share would break the spell of that special moment.'"

"That's what I said, word for word?"

She walked over to stand at her friend's side. Iseabail looked exhausted despite her maid having helped her bathe and braid her hair. "If it is not word for word, it is close. May I hold him?"

Iseabail reluctantly held out the baby and Phoebe took the little bundle into her arms. The new Duke of Nithesdale was the first baby she'd ever held in her life. The birth had been stressful and exhausting. A milestone in their lives she would never forget. Yet it had seemed like an endless bout of pain and pushing and she'd had to lay her trust in the midwife's experienced hands. If Phoebe was honest with herself, she had been scared witless for Iseabail's life and she wasn't certain she would want to put Forrester through such an experience, even if she could have a child. The man would want to throttle someone before the child was born.

She stared down at the peaceful babe in her arms with such a wonderful sense of peace. In that one special moment, it was as if every ugly aspect of life didn't exist. There was no war, no starving children on the streets of London, no violence against those who could not defend themselves. Nothing but this joyous occasion of a boy coming into the world, holding so much promise.

"He is gorgeous. When he grows up, he'll be such a darling all the young debutantes will flock to him, and *you* won't be able to say no to any of his requests."

"He is adorable, isn't he?"

"Yesterday, you were calling him a demon child."

Iseabail's chin rose with the pride of a mother. "Today, I know his true character."

Phoebe returned Xavier to his mother and sat down next to the bed. "In all seriousness, I came here to discuss something with you that needs my attention."

Iseabail's body stiffened. "What's wrong? If something has happened to one of my sisters, you must tell me."

She reached for Iseabail's hand and squeezed it tight. "Your sisters are fine. *Everyone* is fine. Forrester did not want me to tell you, but I told him you needed to know the truth to understand why I must leave."

Iseabail's eyes widened in disbelief. "Leave? Now? You must be joking. I need you here."

"I wish that I were, but it seems that Astley has gotten himself in a spot of trouble."

Relief washed over Iseabail's features. "Astley is always in trouble. It should have been his middle name." She reached over and pulled the little blue blanket with the ducal crest embroidered in gold that she'd made for Xavier tighter around his body.

Phoebe winced. "This is different than his normal rakish naughtiness. He has been taken by Napoleon's men and is being held for ransom."

Iseabail's gaze shot to Phoebe's. "That's not possible. What could Astley have done to end up in the hands of the French?"

"It seems he traveled to America and was on his way back when a French Naval ship captured the American schooner he was on. The ship was captained by Forrester's cousin and he wrote Forrester and asked him to notify Astley's family. He did not want them hearing about it from Napoleon first."

Iseabail's concerned features turned stoic. "Then you must go immediately. Astley may be a rake, but my family owes him everything for saving Caillen's life."

"Are you certain my departure won't be too taxing on you? We should be able to return within a sennight."

"Of course, I am. Xavier and I are fine. Astley's family needs you now."

"You know I would stay with you if I could, but his mother may not trust Forrester arriving with such awful news. She has been through so much, she has a hard time trusting the English. This news of Astley's capture will devastate her."

"I've been too preoccupied with my own family's lack of acceptance by the ton to recognize any slight the earl's family may have received." She hesitated and then asked, "Does the Duke of Ross know?"

"No. Forrester thought Astley's family should hear the news first."

"I understand, and I insist you leave in the morning with Forrester. However, I do have one request before you leave."

"As if you must ask. You know I will do anything in my power to assist you. I value your friendship more than I can possibly say."

"I need assistance with my own resolution."

Phoebe squeezed her hand. "Of course, but the new year is weeks away, can't it wait until our return?"

"No, it can't wait. If we wait, something bad could happen." Iseabail's eyes teared. "Please Phoebe, I need you to bring Forrester in here first. He will resist, but you must insist."

Her brow puckered. "Why?"

Iseabail only said, "Please?"

She sighed and stood up. "What are you up to, Duchess?"

"This was very important to Nithesdale."

"Alright. I will bring Forrester here tomorrow morning before we leave."

Iseabail's bit her lip and shook her head adamantly. "It can't wait. I wish to fulfill a promise, and before you ask what promise, bring your husband-to-be in here."

Not wanting to upset Iseabail further, she agreed. "I will be back with him momentarily."

By the time Iseabail had collected Joshua and convinced him it was not too scandalous to visit Iseabail in her bedchamber, a quarter hour had passed and she wasn't certain Iseabail would be awake. She certainly wanted to be fast asleep in Joshua's arms. He had advised the trip would take two days by coach through the snowy weather. Two days in which he planned to start fulfilling wish number six on her list.

"Do you think we can complete the entirety of my sixth resolution in two days?" she asked.

"I think it will take us a lifetime to fulfill wish six, but it will give us something to look forward to on every coach ride we take." He kissed her then, a kiss that was filled with a promise of so much more.

They ascended the stairs together, their hands inter-twined like an old married couple's as they made their way to the duchess's chamber. Phoebe poked her head in first and found the large canopy bed empty. A quick perusal led her to the adjoining door that stood open.

"Iseabail?"

"I'm in here," she said from the interior of the ducal bedchamber.

Joshua hesitated and she pulled him forward where they found Iseabail sitting by the fire wearing her dressing gown with a blue and gold plaid thrown over her lap. The room had been cleaned and restored to its previous state after the baby's birth. Iseabail was seated in the same chair she had used during her marriage to play chess with Nithesdale.

"Where's the baby?" she asked.

"Mary has taken him to the nursery for a bit."

Unlike most homes of the peerage, Iseabail had relocated the nursery from the opposite wing of the castle to directly across the hall from her room. She had made it perfectly clear to the staff that her child would sleep in her room until the child was at least a year old, and she knew he would be safe.

"I'm sorry there are not enough chairs to go around, so I will get straight to the point. I asked you in here to fulfill my promise to Nithesdale. During his last days he shared several wishes with me. I didn't understand one of his wishes until very recently." She looked back and forth between them. "He wished to see the two of you married. He never told me it was to each other, but he left this for Forrester 'to give his future bride.'"

Iseabail reached for a small silver box that had been sitting in the middle of the chess board since the day of Nithesdale's death. She handed it to Joshua. Phoebe's heart began to race. She looked to the man she loved and longed for something more. She wanted the life that very few people of the ton ever dreamed of having. A life of happiness and love, not duty.

Joshua was one step ahead of her, as if he knew exactly what lay inside the box Iseabail had given him. "His Grace tried to give me this box several years ago. He said a ring wasn't as important as the heart a man gave to a woman, but if I was so caught up in what my bride should wear, I should give her a proper ring. Specifically, his sister's wedding ring."

"Didn't his sister's children want her ring?" Phoebe asked.

Joshua shook his head. "She didn't have any children. She and her husband died shortly after their wedding from a fever. Nithesdale said it was a love match he couldn't deny, but he insisted on a wedding gift of the ring since her betrothed couldn't afford one."

"He never mentioned his sister to me," Phoebe confessed.

Iseabail gave her a sad smile. "It was another loss he didn't want to discuss. Not because he was ashamed of his sister or her merchant husband, but because he loved them both dearly. He believed their love would live on through time. I suspect he believed the two of you shared a similar type of love."

Joshua opened the silver box with the reverence of a man who not only felt the importance of the moment, but the emotion as well. He swallowed hard as he reached in and pulled the ring from where it had sat for a quarter of a century on blue velvet. He gave the box back to Iseabail and before Phoebe knew what he was doing, Joshua sank to one knee in front of her.

"I have loved you for so long, I can't remember a time I didn't care for you with all my heart. It has been the most difficult and rewarding experience of my life. You challenge my mind, heart and body, and I cannot imagine a more perfect woman to spend the rest of my life with. It doesn't matter if we have ten children or none, I will love you for eternity. Phoebe Drake, will you marry me?"

"We already signed a contract."

"I know you wanted a witness. We have one now and a ring."

She studied his earnest expression and saw the truth in his words. Joshua loved her. Not her dowry, not her business. Her. Yet that old doubt still made her hesitate. Again. She glanced at Iseabail who was openly crying. Probably for the man she lost, the man she would never have, and for her fatherless son. But there was also joy—for her. Iseabail saw Joshua's love for her because it was that obvious, and her confidence was all the confirmation Phoebe needed.

"Yes," she whispered. "Yes," she said with more confidence. "Yes!" she shouted and Joshua stood up and took her in his arms. Her feet lifted off the floor as he spun her around, her skirts billowing around her ankles as he kissed her resoundingly. She returned his passionate embrace as their tongues danced a familiar, exhilarating waltz she'd only experienced with him.

A loud throat clearing caused them to laugh, their lips still touching as he slowly lowered her to the floor. Yet their reluctance to part left their foreheads together, silly grins of happiness on their faces.

"You must marry at once," Iseabail declared.

"I agree." Joshua's voice held the same conviction of the duchess's.

"That's impossible. We leave in the morning."

"This is Scotland," Joshua argued.

"I'm aware this is Scotland, but this is our *wedding*," Phoebe implored. She hoped Joshua would understand. Her first wedding had been grand with all the trimmings her parents could imagine, and it meant little. She didn't want a repeat performance, but she wanted a chapel with a vicar. There were no vicars at Caerlaverock.

He raised his hand to her cheek, his dark eyes melting with understanding. "I will do whatever you wish, Phoebe. Just know that I am anxious to begin the rest of our lives together as husband and wife."

"The vicar is here, Phoebe," Iseabail interjected.

She turned to look at her friend. "The vicar is here? But how?"

"I had Paddington send for him because I wanted Xavier to receive his christening while Forrester was still here. I want the two of you to be his Godparents. Would it bother you to have a christening and a wedding on the same day?"

Tears began to fill her eyes. "You want us to be his Godparents?"

"Of course. The duke would have agreed. No one else could be better Godparents for our son than the two of you. Please say yes."

She looked at Forrester, who seemed more shocked by the request than she was, but he gave her a quick nod, and Phoebe replied, "It would be our honour, but are you certain you want to share such a special day with us?"

"If Nithesdale were here he would threaten Forrester with life and limb if he did not make you his wife at Caerlaverock. So, I must insist on his behalf."

Phoebe peered back at Joshua who stood patiently waiting for her reply. "Yes," she said. "I cannot think of a better place to marry the man I love than here, in Nithesdale's home. It will feel as if he is present, giving his blessing."

"Phoebe darling, will you do me the honour of becoming my bride tomorrow morning before we journey to Astley's home?"

More tears flowed down Phoebe's cheeks and she brushed them away. "I would not have it any other way."

Joshua pulled her into his arms once more and whispered in her ear. "Then I expect you to be my wanton wife for the rest of our lives."

"Oh, I plan to be wanton and wicked on our journey because I have a resolution that needs fulfilled."

"It will be *my* pleasure as your husband to assist in the endeavor." Joshua kissed his wanton wife-to-be once more before he picked her up and carried her over the threshold. "We will see you in the church in the morning, Duchess."

"Are you planning to anticipate your vows?" she asked.

"Absolutely," they replied together as the door closed behind them.

The duchess smiled at the painting of her husband and

tipped over her queen on the chessboard. "It seems you played the endgame very well, Your Grace. They fell into each other's arms as you predicted. If I didn't know better, I would say you were nudging them together from beyond the grave."

As she sat alone in her husband's bedchamber, the Duchess of Nithesdale was unaware of the guiding force nudging her toward *her* happily ever after. Instead, she wept —in sadness and in joy, completely lost in her dreams of a duke.

Epilogue

Sir Elias Drake,

Although we have never met, your uncle and my late husband, Lord Richard Drake, always spoke fondly of the fine young man you had become. He often spoke of your work, swearing me to secrecy with each story he related. Your father could not hold back his pride in his son any more than Richard could hold back his pride in you as well. The two of them enjoyed countless nights together extolling your bravery. It is with Richard's sworn oath in mind, I beg your forgiveness for breaking that familial trust. Circumstances of the gravest nature forced my hand, and I alone am responsible for your identity being compromised.

This letter is on behalf of the Countess of Astley. Her son, Simon Clark, the Earl of Astley, has been kidnapped by the French from the American ship, Fairhaven, captained by Miles Gallagher. It is my understanding that Astley was working for the Crown in some capacity and was the primary target of the French. His fate is currently being determined by Napoleon himself.

The countess has your name and direction, but I asked that she keep it in the utmost confidence as I have not shared this with anyone else, including my new husband, as it would put him in a precarious position with other members of the peerage who will be concerned for the earl's safety. The need for discretion has caused me to hide this communication from my husband immediately after taking my vows, but deep in my heart I know you are the one person who can bring the earl home. I only pray my husband forgives me for my lie by omission.

The earl is a rogue with a good heart, and I have recently grown to understand his zeal to live life to its fullest with no apologies given. No one deserves what Bonaparte has done to his own people, certainly not Astley or any other peer of England. Please bring the earl home. He has been dearly missed this holiday season.

Warmest regards,
Mrs. Joshua Forrester,
Formerly Lady Phoebe Drake

—A confidential correspondence written by the former Lady Phoebe Drake to her late husband's nephew, Elias Drake, a privateer sailing The Maribelle on the

Atlantic. The man who will take on the mission of bringing the Earl of Astley home, even if he must marry an unsuspecting scandalous sister and fight Napoleon's most dangerous Hussars to get it done.

A Note from the Author

Dearest Reader,

Thank you for choosing to read *The Wanton Widow*. After the release of *The Ruined Duchess*, many readers requested Phoebe and Joshua's story, and since Phoebe is one of the original ladies to embrace her wanton nature, I felt the Blair sisters would welcome their cousin into *The Scandalous Sisters* fold. A New Year's novella allowed me to give these two deserving characters their very own happily ever after. You will see Phoebe and Joshua throughout *The Scandalous Sisters* series, but this was their time to shine.

Phoebe's family business, Lady Atwood's Millinery was my way of paying homage to bestselling author Margaret Atwood whose profound work, *A Handmaid's Tale*, has somehow found its way to the banned book list. I read it in high school and would still say it was one of the most impactful books of my life.

I hope *The Wanton Widow* gives you a few ideas for your

next fun-filled New Year's resolution. Please read on for a sneak peek into the first two *Scandalous Sisters* novels, *The Ruined Duchess* and *The Rebellious Countess*.

Warmest regards,
Helene

The Ruined Duchess

SCANDALOUS SISTERS BOOK 1

Prologue

In Memoriam of the 7th Duke of Ross, James Edgar Harding

I am highly ~~put upon~~ honoured to be ~~forced~~ permitted by the Royal Historical Society ~~of snobs~~ to record the passing of my ~~depraved~~ loving father ~~not by blood,~~ the 7th Duke of Ross. It is impossible for his countrymen to understand his ~~lack of~~ dedication and sacrifice for the crown. He took a deep ~~personal~~ interest in the financial markets to improve ~~his own~~ the country's coffers. He held the interest of ~~his whores~~ the people at heart and ~~scoffed at~~ exemplified the meaning of self-sacrifice to improve conditions for the poor. He will ~~not~~ be dearly missed by his ~~beast of a~~ doting wife, the Duchess of Ross, and his only ~~bastard~~ son, Nashford Xavier Harding.

—Drafted obituary for James Edgar Harding, 7th

*Duke of Ross, seventeenth day of March 1803 written by
the new, inebriated Duke of Ross, Nashford Xavier
Harding and corrected the next day after he sobered from
his celebratory night of debauchery*

APRIL 1803

"Give it back. I don't want it."

His father's solicitor scurried along behind the new Duke of Ross as he marched through the great hall. "Your Grace, the estate is quite vast."

"It's falling apart. The rugs are threadbare, the furnishings tattered, the walls are dingy with—is that supposed to be art?" His lip turned up at the sight of a child's version of the Corra Linn, one of three waterfalls of Clyde painted directly on the walls in the hall. Before he could take his eyes off the monstrosity, something splattered on his head, seeping through his thick dark hair like an asp slithering through the overgrown fields around the loch.

He closed his eyes. The art wasn't the only ghastly thing occurring in this household. So help him, God, if that was bird shite from doves roosting in the roof, he would get his rifle and blast holes through the birds and the roof.

He looked up at the dripping ceiling and breathed a sigh of relief to discover it was only water saturating his scalp. "And there's rain coming through the roof." The pails scattered around the hall should have made the problem evident. It was shabbiest estate he'd ever seen, and the fields didn't look much better.

"The tenants pay their rent on time, and up until four years ago, the estate was doing quite well."

He stopped, and the barrister nearly ran into his chest as he turned around. As it was, the scrawny man with spectacles slipping down his nose fumbled the stack of papers in his hands. Several floated to the floor as Mr. Bremble swatted at them like a swarm of bees in the garden. He missed every damned one.

"What happened four years ago?"

"The *lady* of the house gave birth, suffered an affliction and never recovered." Bremble crouched to pick up the papers but only succeeded in dropping more of his tiresome reports.

He should help him, calm the man's nerves at the very least. He did neither. He was a duke. "And...?" He didn't see what Mrs. Blair's health had to do with the downfall of an estate. If it had been her husband's health, well, that would be understandable.

"Her...ah...her lover, Mr. Blair, refused to leave her side."

Nash's left eyebrow rose of its own accord. Bremble had caught his attention...for the moment. This was a part of the story he'd somehow missed. It was his understanding Lady Elizabeth Sinclair had scandalized the ton when she'd married a mere mister some fifteen years ago. Mr. Duncan Blair had been a businessman who'd become wealthy at a young age and captured his bride's heart when they were both quite young. The couple had been head over heels in love, according to his own mother, who wouldn't have known love if it bit her in the arse.

He searched his memory for an inkling of a scandal attached to the couple or the estate, but nothing came to mind. The estate had been built in the thirteenth century, or so the story went, and because of its location leading to the Highlands, it had been a vital piece of property to occupy in order to control Scotland. At least that's the way it had been in centuries past. The last battle to occupy Urquhart had been fought in 1689 when supporters of the Protestant monarchy of William and Mary held off the Jacobites. The Protestants subsequently blew the castle to the ground.

From what Nash could see, it should have been left that way.

He didn't want the blasted rubble. He turned away from the man who was trying to tell him he couldn't give back a gift from the king no matter how much he wanted to do so.

He stopped Bremble's tirade with the lift of his hand. "Lady Sinclair was married to Mr. Blair," he corrected the older man.

Bremble shoved his spectacles up the bridge of his nose with his middle finger. "Actually, I was the one to discover the marriage was not legal."

"How is that possible?"

"That I determined it wasn't legal?"

Nash nearly growled, "That the marriage wasn't legal. We're in Scotland."

"But they were married in England."

He was about done with this ridiculous trip. It was a waste of his time. "So, they got married in England. They were *married*."

"No bans were posted and the vicar wasn't a vicar."

"Excuse me?" The man was talking nonsense.

"The couple was in a hurry to marry, and Mr. Blair acquired a special license from a questionable source. A friend of a friend who claimed a favor was due to him by the Crown—it was not. The license was forged. A 'lark' the man confessed. If they had gone a few miles further to Gretna Green the marriage would have been valid, but they stopped in Carlisle where a town drunkard stumbled out of the rectory when they arrived and they mistook him for the vicar."

The story sounded ludicrous. "How could they mistake a drunk for a vicar?"

"In his intoxicated state, the man soiled his own attire and borrowed the real vicar's clothing. Since the vicar was his brother, there was no real crime—until he performed the marriage ceremony."

"You must be joking."

"I'm not, Your Grace."

"You're telling me that a self-made man obtained a forged special license, took his bride-to-be all the way to Carlisle to get married, stumbled across a drunk posing as a vicar, married the society miss, but not really," he had to take a breath before he could continue, "then he traveled to Scotland and lived with her for over a decade as man and wife... and it was only after their deaths that this came to light?"

"Yes, Your Grace."

"How could the man be so stupid and still live?" He winced. The only reason he was here was because the man's own stupidity had caused him to die after becoming so inebriated he fell into the loch and drowned.

"They were said to be in love, Your Grace."

Nash rolled his eyes. It was more likely the man couldn't wait to get under the chit's skirts, and she had been holding out. He had no doubt Blair hadn't actually sat by her side while she succumbed to death and then mourned his wife's passing. It just wasn't done.

Nash knew the greed of self-made men seeking society misses with dowries. Mr. Blair had probably been celebrating his widowhood with whores, and lost track of what was important—his estate. "How did you find out about this?"

"I demanded a copy of the marriage license when Mr. Blair died."

"Why would you do that?"

"Because the duke held a standing IOU from Mr. Blair."

Nash blew out a breath. "Of course he did." Gambling was the one thing his father had done well. That and stealing what belonged to another.

"When I learned of Mr. Blair's death," Bremble continued, "your father instructed me to look into his background."

"I'm beginning to lose my patience, sir. Why would my father care about Mr. Blair's background?"

"I'm getting to that, Your Grace. Since the estate has brought in a tidy sum in the past, I suggested to your father that it could bring in a sizable profit once again if it were managed properly. I have always inquired upon the estates that would bring a tidy profit for the duke when the duke held an IOU. That's how your father acquired so many estates."

God save him from helpful solicitors. The man was more evil than his father.

He sighed and looked around the grand hall. He supposed the castle couldn't be considered a rubble since it was made of ancient stone and it was said to have been fought over repeatedly for its strategic position on the road to Inverness. The view of Loch Ness was passable. Some may want to live in such a place...just not him. It would take far too much of his hard-earned money to repair the castle to its previous glory. He should decline to collect on the IOU and let the heirs of Mr. Blair keep the estate.

It was in his best interest. The road north was treacherous and his coach had thrown two wheels on the journey. He couldn't imagine many of his mistresses wanting to travel to a drafty old castle on a bitterly cold loch which could only boast of a brutal and biting wind. His current mistress, Cecily, had found the trip to be unbearable. Her weak stomach and the frequent stops they'd made to accommodate her had turned it into a tedious three-day trip from Dumfries. It had also made him painfully aware of his need to be closer to London in order get away from the unpleasant side of traveling with a woman. He'd rather travel *to* a woman in the future.

"You're saying Mr. Blair owed my father the price of the estate?"

Bremble shook his head vigorously. "No, Your Grace. Mr. Blair owed your father one hundred pounds."

"One hundred pounds? That's it? Then tell me exactly how I came to acquire the entire estate?" he asked, even though he didn't want the answer.

Bremble nearly preened as he stood up with his papers now neatly stacked in his arms. "Mr. Blair said there was no problem paying the debt, but he died and he didn't have an estate manager to pay his debts. Your father—"

At the sound of Nash's growl, the solicitor cleared his throat and started again. "The previous duke instructed me to advise the Crown of the debt owed, but when the duke passed so suddenly, I was a bit busy to do anything about it. Then the king's man of affairs contacted my firm regarding compensating you for finding the king that wonderful horse. Of course, I remembered the debt, and the lack of a legitimate marriage, and I suggested this piece of property be compensation since it was scheduled to go back to the Crown anyway."

Nash frowned. "Don't the Blairs have daughters? In Scotland, the estate transfers to the daughters if there are no heirs."

"Not to *bastard* daughters, it doesn't."

"Excuse me?" He seemed to be repeating himself, but Bremble didn't mind. If anything, the man was quite pleased to discuss ad nauseam the subject of how he stole the children's birthright.

"Lady Sinclair was not married to Mr. Blair. The six daughters were not born in the marriage bed."

A sick feeling knotted in his gut. "They're bastards," he clarified.

Bremble grinned. "They're bastards."

The man repeating his words made Nash suddenly understand his mistress's weak stomach all too well.

Wailing broke through the air like a clap of thunder rolling through the Highlands. He looked up the stairs to see six sets of eyes staring down upon them. Six orphaned girls. The youngest appeared to be the source of the disturbance and continued with the racket as if someone was pulling her hair out by the roots. From what Nash could see, not one of the other girls standing near her was causing her any pain. If anything, they were attempting to comfort her. Four of the girls became so engrossed in the youngest's despair, they forgot about him and Bremble standing below.

The sixth set of eyes leading the pack, however, told another story. She couldn't have been a day over fourteen and she was ignoring her sisters. She was a child, really, with a wild mass of auburn curls that reflected the untamed flame alight in her green eyes. He knew the color because unlike her younger siblings, this girl was focused on their presence, and from the anger marring her perfect complexion, he'd bet she'd been listening in on their entire conversation.

He met all six girls at the bottom of the steps and bowed. The wailing stopped. "Ladies, forgive me for making your acquaintance without a proper introduction. I am Nashford Harding, Duke of Ross."

All six girls stared at him now. The youngest one sniffled. Her hair was a bit darker than the rest, without a hint of red in the long strands. The four girls consoling her had identical features with pale complexions and blond hair done up to make them look much older than what they actually were. Stick-figures that were currently all legs and arms, but no doubt would have captured many a buck's attention if they were introduced to society when they came of age—which would never happen, thanks to him and the imbecile standing next to him.

It was the oldest one, however, who captured his attention. On the cusp of womanhood, she was a mere shadow of her future self. No doubt by the time she reached her majority, she would be the type of woman to command the attention of every man when she made her way into a ballroom. He could imagine her storming the entrance and causing such a disturbance, the ton could only stand by in awe of her tempest spirit. Fire glistened in her auburn curls, and upon closer inspection, it seemed to hold every shade of her siblings's hair. As if the younger girls were but a small glimmer of her perfection...

...And she would no longer be allowed to enter society. Thanks to him.

At the age of twenty, he was a duke. The title and responsibilities were his alone. No one would ever be the wiser to his true birth...and in turn, he had repaid the kindness of fate by ruining the lives of six young girls, all in the span of one month.

Bloody hell.

The Rebellious Countess

SCANDALOUS SISTERS BOOK 2

Prologue

Dear Sir Williamson,

Much to my ~~horror~~ chagrin, I find myself ~~facing a firing squad~~ married. The Scotch merchant would not allow ~~a Sassenach pirate~~ an Englishman to purchase his liquor. He said~~, and I quote, "Tek yer honkin' Sassenach arse away til ye marry a wee bonnie lass of good breeding." Translation,~~ if I didn't marry a Scottish lady and quickly, I would not be able to purchase the Scotch needed to bribe the ~~wicked witch~~ tavern keeper at The Happy Hag. Without that Scotch, the ~~damnable~~ Hag refused to set up my meeting. Without a ~~blasted virgin~~ bride, the entire plan to recover the package would be ruined.

In this particular region, ladies of quality are ~~bloody~~ difficult to find. When I happened across one in town, I ~~knocked over two lads and their grandfather~~ managed to obtain an introduction. As gratuitous as it may sound, it turned out to be a ~~disaster~~ minor problem. I did not know the identity of her brother by marriage until after I proposed, and by then it was too late to find another bride. Yet with no alternatives, I had to make a decision which ~~would~~ could create a ~~war violent enough for Robert the Bruce to dig out of his grave to fight~~ bit of a scandal.

The young lady's sister is the Duchess of Ross, bride to none other than, Nashford ~~bloody~~ Harding, ~~the bastard~~ Duke of Ross. Unfortunately, the duke and I are previously acquainted. ~~He broke my damned nose when he discovered me in a compromising position with a lady.~~ I will leave the details of our acquaintance to your imagination, but it is safe to say it was over ~~his mother~~ a woman he held in the highest esteem.

I have no doubt the duke will be in contact with you shortly, if he has not already. Please know, the plan was to leave her in Dumfries, ~~disappointedly~~ untouched, but then the seller wanted to meet the lass at the docks and I had no choice but to take my ~~bloody~~ wife aboard The Maribelle. When we arrive in Le Conquet I will send the ~~temptress~~ young lady to Plymouth immediately. ~~The siren~~ She may be a bit confused as to her identity, since I had to use an alias. She will probably shed ~~fathoms of~~ a few tears and claim to be Lady Máira Collins, Countess of Dorset. If you could ~~take the damned shackles off my ankles~~ arrange for an annulment upon her return, I would greatly appreciate the assistance. I will keep her safe from the crew and myself ~~hopefully~~ throughout the voyage. She is a ~~passionate~~ spirited girl who could use *some assistance finding a husband after everything she has endured ~~from me~~ for her country.*

My apologies for the ~~black eyes the duke will deliver~~ difficulties this will create. You have my word as a ~~rogue who wants nothing more than to introduce Miss Blair to the sweetest carnal delights this side of heaven~~ gentleman, she is untouched.

When our package is secured, I will send word.

~~Pray that I can honor my word,~~

Regards,

E

—An edited draft report to Sir Robert Williamson, War Office London, England, from an unidentified agent of the Crown, Dumfries, Scotland. It was written while the agent angrily awaited a Scottish smuggler and edited later that night as he stared at his wife's unconscious form lying across his captain's bunk aboard his ship, The Maribelle. Her undefiled breasts nearly bursting from the neckline of her wedding gown was a display that would tempt the best of men—especially men like him.

This was her life. She was on the honeymoon trip of a debutante's dreams. Passionate kisses, festive glasses clinking, raucous laughter spilling through the seams of the building and...

...A drunken sailor falling at her feet.

"Ummpf." His fetid breath filled the air and the condition of his rotting teeth made a shudder crawl through her body when he rolled over and grinned at the sight of her. "Beggin' yer pardon, missy." Suggestive eyebrows waggled, and the *gentleman* tipped an imaginary hat on his head, his two front teeth displaying more filth than she'd seen in her lifetime.

She cringed and scooted further under the table. Cheap ale spilled over the edges, filth covered the floor where she cowered like a…a rat? A gasp was torn from her lips. Was that a rat?

Drat and double drat! She crossed her arms over her knees and brought the skirts of her soiled wedding gown closer to her body. Her safe haven should have been the strong arms of her gorgeous husband wrapped around her body as she playfully dodged his public advances. Instead, she was shooing away a beady-eyed rodent who only stared at her as if *she* were the one who needed to vacate the premises.

The rat, on second thought, was much more appealing than the two-faced, good for nothing blackguard she'd married. That *rat* had abandoned her on the docks with no money, no luggage, and no way to find her way home. Just some cryptic message passed on by a member of his crew as he'd pointed down the street of the dockside town.

"Talk to Hag. She'll give you passage."

It was as if Ellison had dropped her off in a foreign land to be rid of her once and for all. She hadn't even had her wedding night…

No. The only passionate kisses she'd witnessed were

between the buxom barmaid and the beaver-toothed sailor currently crawling on his hands and knees toward the exit. Máira winced as a handful of the barmaid's strawberry blonde hair dropped to the floor and got lost in the shuffle and scuffle of the men fighting throughout the tavern.

The woman cursed, glass shattered and sprinkled to the floor in a storm of profanity. "May the devil take ya, ya dirty ol' rum gagger." A man staggered in front of her, his boots kicking the ball of hair closer to Máira.

"How did my honeymoon end in The Happy Hag tavern in France? France! Aren't we at war with France?" Máira asked.

Her question went unanswered. No shock there. Like the last several days, she was the last person on anyone's mind. From the time she awoke aboard a ship, she had one alarming experience after another. There had been no plans to board a ship on their honeymoon. There had been no plans to meet a pirate. And there certainly had been no plans to end up in the middle of a brawl in a bloody tavern in France.

To make matters worse, every rotten thing that occurred to her could be traced back to the moment she had said "I do" to the Earl of Dorset, the bloody blackguard who'd ignored her the entire voyage to France. A voyage that should have taken less than a day but had been interminably long. On the very first day, she'd been lost and disoriented. With each roll of the waves, her stomach had done three. When lightning cracked and thunder roared, she'd sworn her head split in two and bounced off the walls. Her roaring megrim evidence of her being stuck in a hellish nightmare. She'd finally crawled out of the cabin and to the ladder to make her way to the deck. The rain then pelted her face and soaked her dress like a second skin to her body. As she'd shielded her face with her hands and looked up to the where she thought a captain of a ship might be—there *he* stood, wearing pirate clothes. *Pirate clothes.*

If her face had any color to it at all, it leached from her cheeks when she looked around and saw the hard men manning the decks. It only proceeded to get worse when her husband's beautiful head of hair turned in her direction and his handsome face delivered an angry scowl. His icy glower held enough menace to pierce her heart with ten daggers, like the one he wore strapped at his waist. In that moment, she felt a fear like nothing she'd felt in her life, and she'd felt plenty of fear before boarding that ship. Her life had not been made of tea cakes and fripperies.

Yet the gorgeous, strapping, sweet, doting Earl of Dorset who had worshiped the ground she walked while they'd been on dry land in Dumfries, had turned into a cold, arrogant bastard pirate aboard ship. A bastard who leapt over the railing onto the deck in front of her before she could run back to her cabin and bolt the door.

"What the hell are you doing up here?" he'd bellowed. It could have been rain splattering on her face, but she'd imagined it to be angry spittle. That, along with her sudden memory of her older sister Iseabail lecturing her, "You can't possibly know him well enough to marry him!" had been enough to make her toss her accounts all over his shirt. She'd waited for a backhanded blow that never came.

Instead, he'd looked down at his shirt, rolled his eyes, and ripped it from his body. One minute it was there, and the next she was staring at the broad expanse of a naked chest with too much muscle. Flawless skin sculpted into the ideal embodiment of the male species. Michelangelo would curse his perfection.

"Bloody hell," she cursed his perfection.

Ellison blinked at the profanity, then tossed her over his shoulder like a basket of fish.

She hadn't fought him. She'd let him carry her below deck, into the cabin she'd occupied where he unceremoniously tossed her onto the bed and left her without another word. Then he'd bolted the door shut—from the outside! The ship had rocked and swayed violently as she'd stared at the door. If it took on water, she'd go down to Davey Jones' locker without anyone the wiser. Despite knowing the furious pirate was the same man she'd married, she hadn't recognized the man who'd secured her in a room with no lifeline. He hadn't the time, nor the inclination, to deal with his sick wife.

She had hoped things would change, return to normal when they'd docked in the port of...port of...bloody hell. She didn't even know what port she was in and now she was cursing like the sailors around her. Would she have to fight as well?

A man bent over and looked under the table, his eyes met hers and her blood curdled under his scrutiny. His coat was clean, his trousers that of a nobleman, and his manners gave the appearance of a gentleman as he reached out to take her hand. Only a fool would believe he meant to rescue her from the melee. And despite the evidence to say otherwise, Máira was no fool. She scooted back in the corner, pushing the rat out of his home, and the man's grin grew.

"You like it rough, *chérie?*" His aristocratic polish and refined English were completely out of place with the street-born curses of the Frenchmen fighting around them. Yet deep in her marrow, Máira recognized the evil within. Not for one moment did she believe they would bond over shared nationalism. This man was evil down to his toenails.

"I will make you scream and beg for mercy," he cooed.

He thought she was French and didn't understand. To a naive miss who didn't speak English, he would probably appear as a debonaire gentleman coming to her rescue. Máira knew differently. She understood more than she cared to. His brown eyes spoke of a lost, soulless man who hadn't felt anything other than disdain for another human being in years, if ever.

He lunged for her ankle and she screamed, but there was too much noise for anyone to hear. She kicked and punched, striking him on the temple which only seemed to feed his violence as he dragged her out from under the table and wrenched her arm behind her back. She screamed once more, as her face slammed into the floor.

"I'll teach you to strike your betters, bitch." She felt his breath on her ear as he attempted to slam her face against the floor a second time, but she twisted her body, sacrificing her shoulder as her arm wrenched higher.

A scream vibrated through the air and Máira wasn't sure if she was screaming or someone else was making the unholy noise. Her attacker's grip went suddenly slack and he fell onto his belly next to her. Arms underneath his chest and his head turned to the side, he looked directly at her. He didn't smirk, or talk, or even crawl away on his knees. He laid there bleeding with a knife the size of Cook's meat cleaver buried in one sightless eye.

Máira bit the back of her hand to hold the scream in her throat. She had never seen a man die before. She had experienced tragic loss multiple times, but this was gory and horrifying. Tears of blood streamed across the bridge of his nose and cheek and down onto the floor.

She wished the man at her side was her husband—the dirty Lothario who'd left her to this fate. *This* was what her sister had warned her about, the life of a woman who took a chance and married a stranger.

Bloody Hell. "I swear I'm going to kill him."

About the Author

After following her childhood dream to serve and protect, Helene retired from public service and began a new dream— creating happily ever afters. First publishing in mystery and romantic suspense, she decided to add her love of travel and history to her personal oeuvre. From the first page to the last, Helene promises to take you on a journey to arouse your imagination and capture your heart.

When she's not writing or researching her next novel, she can be found rummaging through antique stores, estate sales, and flea markets looking for that next piece of inspiration.